THE SURPRISE
AUCTION

THE SURPRISE
AUCTION

Ruth Giles

Library of Congress Control Number:		2021903145
ISBN:	Hardcover	978-1-6641-8516-6
	Softcover	978-1-6641-8515-9
	eBook	978-1-6641-8514-2

Print information available on the last page.

Rev. date: 07/20/2021

To order additional copies of this book, contact:
Xlibris
844-714-8691
www.Xlibris.com
Orders@Xlibris.com
828702

CONTENTS

CHAPTER 1

The Auction

The auctioneer speaks quickly—and when you can make out what he's saying, he's sold the item that interests you the most.

I have twenty-five, can I get thirty, YES! I got thirty, now can I get thirty-five and now forty! I got forty, now forty-five, I got forty-five, who would give fifty? I got fifty, do I hear sixty? Sixty, do I hear seventy? I got sixty, now can I get seventy, seventy anybody? How about sixty-five? Can I get sixty-five, sixty-five, now can I get sixty-five? Anybody, can I get sixty-five, I got sixty now sixty-five, sixty-five? Anyone, going once, going twice! SOLD! For sixty dollars.

At daybreak, it was a cool and invigorating morning, full of songbirds chirping in the wind, and it happened one crisp August day. With great anticipation, I Starling Rose, has been waiting and saving for this day for several months. Aha! Today IS the day! The morning temperature was hovering in the seventies all ready, with just a breeze to carry the perfumed aroma of my flowers that I had planted out in front of my house, with vibrant colors of burnt orange marigolds, lemon yellow pansies, and the pristine white daisies. I grew each one from seeds since potted plants were too expensive for my budget. I love to sit on the front porch and watch a new day begin as I drink my morning coffee. However, this day is special, and I am full of excitement. I am going to an auction. I know going to an auction does not sound too exciting for some, but I look forward to finding some treasured items that was once someone's pride and joy.

I, Starling Rose, already in my 30's has had my share of difficulties and challenges in life. I have been trying to get on the right track of being a successful mother of two lovely children and offer them the necessities in their life. My life's journey has experienced a few challenges and with God's help I have gotten through the hurdles. Today I am putting *myself* at the top of my list by doing something that is of interest to me.

I am headed out to an auction. "Yippee" I uttered. This is not just any auction. I can almost hear the chant of the auctioneer as he rattles off the numbers and each one higher than the last. It is being held at the home of a deceased family estate on a back road outside Richwood, Ohio. I was not quite sure how to get there, but I found it by following the signs erected by the auctioneer. The back road was rutted and narrow with grassy patches here and there and almost impassable on a tree-shaded rural roadway. My youngest brother, Allen, had given me directions. He loved to go to auctions too, so he became an auctioneer. Supporting my brother as an auctioneer is one of my prerogatives, plus I love all the unique things I find.

By following the auction signs, plus I spotted a bunch of vehicles along the roadway, I knew it was just up ahead. Now to find a place to park. I do not like to park along the road because I am afraid of someone sideswiping my car, so I drove up into the residence, and they were parking cars in a field behind the barn. Oops! Someone pulled out from in front of the barn, so I parked there in front of the tall weeds. This spot was much closer to the house and the auction tables. Guess I was lucky this time. Here I am, Ms. Starling, ready to take part in this Special Auction and all the unique items that I can find there. It gave me a proud feeling knowing my brother was the auctioneer. I try to live every day of my life as an adventure and approach all aspects of my life as an event. Life has tried to knock that spirit out of me, but I always have faith that things will get better.

"I made it here! Yippee" I blurted out, but no one was there to hear me. Most of the people were walking around checking out all the items for sale.

Spotting Lynn on her way to the auction trailer, I waved to her while getting out of my car. Lynn is my sister-in-law and married to Allen, brother number five, who is the auctioneer. She is a warmhearted person and has been a gem to our family.

"Hey there!" she hollered, as she got closer, and hollering back to her, I added, "I am attending this auction on my own today! Could not get anybody to come with me."

She responded, "Oh no you're not, your son is here helping so at least some of your family is here." Lynn is such a caring and understanding person and has worked wonders for my little brother, Allen. He wanted to become an auctioneer, and she helped him pursue his goal in his life by persuading him to go to an auctioneering school.

I have had a passion for going to auctions since I was ten. I can remember one time I went with my dad when he just happened to see an auction along his way. My brother David was with us, and he was a year older than me. This was a country auction of someone who had passed away, and I believe these are called estate auctions. Dad reminded us to never put your hand up for anything . . . because they think you want to buy it. And if you cannot pay for it, they keep you committed, and you must work for it until it is paid for. He made it sound cruel and evil if you happen to put your hand up to bid on something. Boy, talk about putting fear into a young child, he surely did.

He mumbled, "Now we cannot buy anything today. We are just going to look around. You can walk around and look, but I want you to keep me in your sight all the time. Do you understand? Daddy is going out and look at the tools."

I whispered, "Yes, I do," and David snickered, "Okay." I told him that I just wanted to look at the boxes of stuff. "We won't put our hand up for anything, Daddy. We will just look," I replied with a little bit of fear in my voice.

It was amazing when he went and got a bidding number since he told me he could not buy anything. Guess he thought we wouldn't notice.

With lots of excitement, we would go and look at the box lots and check out the boxes of toys and books and records that were segregated into each box. Some of them were very enticing, but I had no money to buy anything, so I went on to the next box and fantasized about owning all the boxes of my selections. Someday, my dream may come true. Dad never bought anything, and we were only there about an hour.

There are usually lots and lots of people at public auctions, looking for a good deal or finding treasures of some special memory that they experienced. You'd see a lot of farmers and Amish men at auctions in their aging rubber boots and dirt-infused jeans or bib overalls because there might be a specific tool that they need or something they could not do without.

There are antique dealers too, awaiting to find that unique masterpiece of an old item that they think would be worth hundreds of dollars. If you have deep enough pockets, you can buy almost anything your heart desires at an auction. And there are the ordinary, just like me, looking for something to enhance my home and someone that just loves to attend auctions. In addition to my youngest brother, Allen, who is the licensed auctioneer, I have two other brothers that like to attend auctions too. David, our eldest who grew up to be a frugal kind of person and Carl, brother number four, who likes to live the simple and economical life but can also be frugal and thrifty at times. David was just a year and two weeks older than me.

Sometimes I would get my daughter Patty to come with me. I am sure, since she is a teenager, they may be boring to her. She is my one and only daughter with blue eyes and her strawberry-blonde hair and a temper to go along with it. She is a tomboy just like I was growing up. She always joined me in rummaging through the box-lot items that catches my attention. She is my second child and very empathetic at times but very open-minded. She would literally explore the items in the box to see what was in there that she might want as if she was looking for buried treasure.

When Mother could, she loved to go with me too. She always wanted to be up front close to the auctioneer, so Allen could see her. Mother always got bidding number one, and Allen would always recognize Mom to the crowd when she was there. She would occasionally get embarrassed a little and laugh at what he said. He called her his number one fan and that she was for sure.

Mother was very patient most of the time and a caring person after having ten children to care for. She always enjoyed helping others by offering her services of cleaning houses when she was needed. I think that ever since mother was a little girl, she knew that she was put on this earth to be a wife and mother, and that is exactly what she chose to do. Mother lived for her children and always put herself last.

As I got out of the car and was walking up to the auction, I could smell a great aroma of hay fields, barn smells, and the smell of the abandon chicken coups. Oh! What a unique little farm this was at one time, with fields of clover all around it. There was grass-lined stepping stones leading up to the back door of the house. Along with a big two-story barn, there was a garage, a shed with corn cribs on each side, and a big farmhouse all weathered with time to a grayish white. The house had several rose bushes of various colors, looked like some four o'clocks growing along the front porch, some beautiful zinnias and mums just reaching for the sunshine among the tall weeds, and several hostas that mingled between them. The house was a faded white, two-story, with a medium-sized porch on the front and a wooden swing hanging from the rafters. There was a big enclosed porch on the back and a well pump outside. You could smell the stagnant water from the pump. It must work because there was water in the cement basin that lay under the pump. Such a tranquil and cozy home. I have often heard, if walls could talk, what would they say? I am sure there were many adventures from those who dwelled in this house for it feels like a warm hug, as if those walls were embracing and protecting them through their life's journey. The old house, with its centuries-settled foundations, brought a feeling of welcome to those that visited and dwelled within.

A clothesline was attached to the side of the house with a T post holding up the other end. Mother once told me that you can read a person's home life by the clothes they have on their clothesline. If there are blue jeans or bib overalls, it means that there is a man in the house. If there are children's clothes, it means there are little ones in the family; and if there are aprons, it means there is a hard-working mother living here. If there are sheets and pillowcases on the line, it means that she likes to keep a tidy home. Some of my happiest childhood memories were hanging out the laundry with Mother. She would put all the socks together, all the shirts and jeans together, all the underwear. Maybe this was to help make the folding of the clothes easier. I remember Barb, sister number two, always told Mom to put her underwear behind a shirt or something so people couldn't see her underwear as they drove by. I would help her by handing her the clothes pins until I got tall enough to reach the clothesline. Then I had to hang them up by myself. This soon became quite a chore since there were usually ten to twelve people she washed clothes for.

Our life has many changes, some with painful consequences and some with rewarding experiences. It is all worth it if you have learned from the changes. I wonder what kind of lady lived in this house.

There was an abundance of auction tables spread out over the newly mowed lawn that was once covered with dandelions. The old house brought the perspective of passing years in a world that had accelerated by the changing of times.

I spotted Lynn, Allen's wife, in the auction trailer that was located close to the back door of the house, and she was assigning and passing out numbers. I have not gotten my number yet. I was ready to show my driver's license to get a bidding number. That reminds me, this is one of the first things you should do when going to an auction.

I kiddingly remarked to Lynn, "You can give me my winning number now." She jokingly replied, "You will have a winning number if the price is right when you make your purchases."

"Yell, that makes sense."

I got number 25 so I thanked her and added, "Thanks for giving me the number that is my age."

She replied, "DON'T YOU WISH!"

I asked her, "Are there any neat things here?"

"It depends on what you are looking for," she answered. "There are some nice quilts and crocheted items and, of course, you like baskets. There is a big box of them and there is a box of records. I have not had a chance to see if there are any Elvis. Go look around because the auction doesn't start for forty-five minutes."

I bid her farewell and was ready to find my valuable souvenirs.

So I moseyed on over to the tables, my card in my back pocket with the pencil. The bidding number card they had was unique. You could write the items you were interested in on one side of the card then write what you bought and the price you bid on the other side. Your number was at the top in large print. Perhaps this is a day of dreams seeping into reality. I wonder what amazing treasures I will find today.

As I was wandering around the property, I spotted off in a distance, but still inside the fence row, some beehives off to one corner of the backyard. There must have been five or six hives. These pollinators may sting, but they do honey-sweet things for us. Their wings glimmer like the surface of ruffled ice, reflecting the bright August sunlight. The honey will taste of the clover that fills the meadows nearby and brighten every morning right through winter. Every time I see a bee flying by on their way to pollinate and make honey, I am reminded of what little miracles of evolution they are and say a little prayer of thanks that He made them possible in His world. I do not like to kill the honeybees. I just swat at them and hope they leave me alone.

It reminds me, as I strolled along the backyard, of the times we respond to the greatest gifts in ways that perplex the guardian of nature.

There were plants such as clover, plants that feed the bees, that keep alive the very insects we need. The remains of a garden creation still held the dried-up tomato vines. In her once beautiful flower bed, there were the daisies, a few poppies, and other wildflowers that once grew along the garden fence. Bees loved the flowers; birds loved the seeds. Close by was a blackberry bush with a few berries that lingered as they were soaking up the warm rays of the sunshine. Nature has her quiet way of giving if we are willing to see the gifts she bestows.

I got to thinking about the auction, although it had not started yet. I love all the excitement and anticipation of whether my bid will be the winning bid. Or how much is this item worth, and do I need it, and did I get a bargain on the item? Almost like playing the lottery, but you have a better chance of winning the bid at an auction. It is all too easy to get caught up in auction fever and bid far more than you intended.

There are many types of auctions, from estate auctions, minimum bid auctions, reserved auctions, and absentee auctions. The last one you can bid even if you cannot attend the auction in person. I guess I am more favorable to the estate auctions, the ones wherein the items are out on tables and you can walk around and look at them before the auction starts. You can check out all the box-lot contents and rummage through the trinkets and treasures that are in it. This way you have an idea of what you are buying, what is in a box, and what makes it so unique that you want to bid on. Occasionally, you get those bidders rearranging the box lots to suit themselves and putting the items that interest them in the box they want to bid on. I know this is not supposed to happen, but I have witnessed it on some occasions. I try to set a maximum amount of what I want to spend on my selected items, but sometimes it is hard to not go beyond that total.

I was so excited when my little brother Allen decided to take up auctioneering as a side job. I should say younger brother because he is around six feet tall and quite handsome. He did not need the money because he had a great job at the local auto manufacturing company. He just had a love for talking fast like auctioneers do. Sometimes I think another reason is since he was the youngest of ten kids, being an auctioneer requires people to listen to him. He could reach down deep in his voice box and make a sound that people would pause at what they were doing and wonder where that sound came from. He would say, ALL RIGHT! LISTEN UP! Honestly, I think he scared people into listening to him. He was a good auctioneer and very considerate of his audience. If there were several older people, he would talk a little bit slower and distinct. If there were younger ones, he would do his chant and rattle off the numbers real fast and the item was sold before you knew what was selling.

Allen's son, Bud, and my son, Brian, would occasionally help with the auctions by holding up the items being bid on. They would watch the audience and holler "YEP" when they got a bid to let Allen know to go higher.

I did not have much to spend today, but working two jobs, I saved till I had some extra money. I had fifty dollars to spend. I worked in the office at a local fertilizer company and sometimes in a restaurant in the evening waiting tables. After going through two unsuccessful marriages, I had two kids to raise by myself, there was hardly any extra money to do anything. I know that I am going to do everything I can for my children because I want to be able to say I'm doing a good job with no regrets.

As I was walking around and checking out the box lots, Allen came up behind me and then got in my face and shouted my name, "SISTER STARLING!" He scared me a little bit, then he laughed at me because he could see that he frightened me. Another successful trait he was proud of.

He asked, "Did you bring lots of cash?"

I chimed in, "I did not bring a lot, but I am prepared to bid on some of the things."

Allen remarked, "They got lots of box lots here, which you like."

"Yes, I see that and there are a lot of people here. Looks like a good turnout," I told him. "I want to start to check out all the box lots. Do you need some help with the auction? I could hold up the items as they were selling."

He replied, "Brian and Bud are here to help." He told me he had to get going as the auction would be starting soon.

First, I looked at the box lots. Box-lot items are when they put a lot of the same or similar items in a box and sell the whole box for one money. I can usually find something of value to me or someone else with box-lot items. You can find treasured and trashed items in box lots. There were some forty-five records in a box, so I rummaged through every one of them to see if there were any Elvis Presley, but there was none.

Moving on to the other tables, I spotted some unique baskets which I liked to collect, and there were several of assorted sizes in one big box. There was one that looked like a picnic basket with two lids that opened toward the middle. I rummaged farther down in the box and spotted one purple basket, another pink, and they looked like unique baskets. I added them to my number of items to bid on, on my bidding card. I wondered if the baskets were this lady's children's Easter baskets. They both resembled each other but in different colors. There were a few berry baskets that looked new, but still had the stains in them from the berries. In the bottom were three holiday tins with various scenes on the lid. Yes, this big box of basket goes on my list of things to bid on.

There was a box that was full of silverware. Lots and lots of silverware. Lots of different patterns of spoons, knives, and forks, plus several unique kitchen items. *Hmm, this box is interesting. I wondered if there were any complete table service per say, for four to six people. May have to bid on it*, I mumbled to myself, so I added it to my card.

As I was ready to move on, I noticed some black tarnish on my hands. Probably came from the silverware. I know that everything in that box looked like it was dirty. It looked like it was coal dust or stove ashes. Several other items were tarnished and dirty. Well, to avoid getting that black stuff on my white shorts, I had to be careful what I touched. I wonder how I would get all that black stuff and rust off the silverware and things. That is okay, I can probably clean them by soaking them in a pan with a bottle of coke. *If coke can clean this off, just imagine what it does to your stomach*, I thought. There were some napkins on a table, so I took them over to the water hose that was wound around a car tire rim. There was enough water left in the hose for me to clean off my hands. Those silverware and things must have been sitting around for a while. I remember another recipe for removing tarnish is baking soda, salt, and vinegar. One of them should work. From looking at the content of this box, I believe it was a catch-all box. It contained two of those plastic silverware dividers, and they each were plum full of silverware and miscellaneous kitchen items.

Of course, there was the usual box lots of household items of used pots and pans and a couple electric skillets. There were several various sizes of table and desk lamps. There was a box of cookbooks that looked inviting. I love looking at old cookbooks. You can get some tasty recipes from them. I must come back to that and check it out, so I added the cookbooks to my card of things to bid on.

I remembered when I first took up residence in this area after my first divorce, I used to go to the Plain City Auction House that was held the last Friday of each month. This had two rooms of stuff and an auction going on in each room. One room had household and kitchen trinkets, and the other one had bigger items like couches and chairs and tables and stands. I found some end tables and a coffee table there when I first came to call Marysville my home. The coffee table looked like a half of an old wagon wheel on each end, and it looked like the wagon bed on top. Rather unique I thought. They sold things so fast there, so you had to be on your toes and pay attention all the time. This auction started at five in the afternoon and went till midnight sometimes.

After walking away from the box-lot tables, I noticed there was a rototiller that looked interesting. I could sure use one of those for my flower beds and my garden. It was stashed behind a bunch of shovels. Spotting my brother Carl standing by a shed close by it, I walked over to him.

I asked Carl, "can you check out this tiller? I need your opinion of value and to see if it works." Carl pulled it out onto the grass and started it. "Yeah! It started!"

He advised, "This is a nice tiller. It has been well taken care of," he reported.

I asked him, "So, Carl, how much do you think it is worth?"

He replied, "Well, around one hundred fifty to two hundred dollars, but you don't know how many people would be interested in buying it."

I remarked, "Well, Carl, I do need one but cannot afford that much money for one, but thanks for your help."

Carl came back with. "Just wait and see what it will bring when it is auctioned." I sighed, as I rolled my eyes at him and mumbled okay. I believe Carl liked auctions just as much as I did.

Carl, being brother number four of the five, was very prosperous in his life because he owned his own electrical business. He was about six feet tall and quite handsome, I think.

I walked around to the other tables and checked out the other items and found some little things I liked but did not necessarily need. There were a couple boxes full of specialty dishes. The dishes you serve food in, with unique designs on them. *These might be antiques*, I thought. So hopefully I can bid on the less expensive items since my funds were limited.

The sun was beginning to warm me up along with everyone else there. I was glad I wore shorts and a T-shirt so the warm breezes could keep me cool. However, there were not many trees in this backyard other than the big oak tree that shaded and hung over most of the backyard. The blue sky was dotted with fluffy white clouds that drifted lazily in the gentle breeze. You could see remnants of what used to be a vegetable garden in one corner of the backyard. Along the walkway was several bushes of flowers. At one time I am sure they were beautiful and adorned the backyard. Due to neglect, they had lots of weeds in them as they tried to emerge and survive.

Well, the main auction was about to start promptly at 10:00 a.m. with Allen reading the rules to abide by when a sale is made.

"All sales are final and become the responsibility of the buyer!" Allen shouted. "You have until one hour after the last item was sold to make sure your items are removed once you have paid for them." He announced that there was a barn full of farm machinery and tools that was supposed to sell starting promptly at one. So that is why there were lots of farmers here. He went on and told of some other rules of the auction, but my mind drifted to the items I wanted to bid on.

He started with the dishes. Some were sets and some were mismatched and some were collector's items. Well, I did not see any dishes that interest me. Then pots and pans and on and on until he came to my box of baskets that I wanted. So, with great anticipation, I am ready to start bidding. I did not want to start the bid. Allen started out the bid at ten dollars then five dollars, then he jumped down to one dollar, someone bid 50 cents, then back up to a dollar. Well, I could go better than that, so I bid two dollars, then there was two fifty, then three. I jumped back in at three fifty and then there was a bid for four dollars, then I bid four fifty. I heard, "Anyone give me five dollars. Five dollars, anyone?" Then no one else would bid on them. Oh wow! I heard, "SOLD for four fifty!"

I GOT IT! I GOT IT! I chanted to myself. I was so excited that it made me eager to bid on more items. I mumbled to myself, *I just love it when a plan comes together. Thank you, Lord!*

After marking it down on my card for four dollars and fifty cents, I am ready to move on to the other items. *They were incredibly unique baskets,* I thought. As I had seen before, there were some with lids, one with a lid on each side, something like a picnic basket. There were some with no lids and some with colored bands around them, and the pink and purple oblong baskets with handles. They were not the Longaberger baskets, but they were well made. I was so proud that I had gotten them. Okay, I need to calm down and pay attention.

Moving on there were cookie jars, mismatched canister sets, candy dishes, old radios, clocks, numerous toasters, and other items. Some of these things were antiques and some were just junk. I should not call it junk; they are treasuresto someone.

There were several flower vases, flower stands, and flowerpots. I found a big clear glass vase and thought this one would be nice to take flowers over to the church. It was big at the bottom and smaller at the top, and it had some gold paint around the rim. This one I might bid on if it is not too much. I waited patiently as people were buying up the items that interested them.

He will start selling the vases next, I whispered to myself. He asked the ladies standing there if there was any one vase, they were interested in. He would sell it separate. There were two ladies that were wanting to bid on some unique-looking vases. One was green and the other was pink. I believe these would be antiques since they were depression glass.

There were several milk glass vases and bud vases. Well, I do not need any antique vases. He put the two vases side by side and announced, "These two vases I guess are called depression glass. They will be sold by choice or two times the money." I watched the ladies bid back and forth. He started them out at twenty dollars then down to ten and one lady shouted yes!

Then he said, "How about fifteen?" and the other lady held up her card, so I believe that was a yes for her. "I've got fifteen, now I've got fifteen! Ladies!"

Then the other lady muttered, "Twenty," and Allen yelled, "I got twenty, do I hear twenty-five?" and the other lady said, "I bid thirty dollars," and he looked at the other lady and chimed in, "I got thirty now, do I hear forty?" and she shook her head yes.

Then Allen reported, "How about forty-five?" and she shook her head no. "I've got forty, now forty-five." I heard Allen say, "SOLD FOR FORTY DOLLARS!" And he pointed to the lady that had bought them. She took both of them.

For forty dollars apiece. And they are collector's items, I told myself. Okay, this made me nervous. Will that one vase bring that much?

The lady that bid on the vases had walked away. The lady that won the two depression glass vases left with a big smile on her face. She whispered, "They will match my set of dishes I already have at home." Well now that was nice that she could add to her collection, I thought.

Now he was auctioning off more vases. There were several smaller vases, and some were that dark blue that was pretty, and there were some red ones and some medium-sized clear glass ones and of course the milk glass ones. After some deliberation, he could not get anyone to bid on the smaller ones, so Brian found a box and he and Bud put them in it. There must have been six or eight of them that were of various sizes.

"Now, let us bid on this box of vases. All of them for one money." Silence was all around me. No one would bid on the box of vases. So he set them aside and next he commented, "Now here is one big vase! This will hold lots of your flowers, ladies." I heard the ladies chuckle a little.

He started it out at twenty-five, then fifteen, then ten. No one was bidding on it. That is unusual because it seems like the items I want, everyone else does too. I added, "Five dollars!"

He hollered, "I got five dollars, now six, do I hear six, anyone?" No one answered or held up their hand. So no one wanted it but me. He yelled, "SOLD to this lady for five dollars." Then he asked me if I wanted the box of vases for one dollar and I immediately answered yes, YES!

Well, what just happened here? I suckered myself into that one fairly good, as I thought to myself. After people walked away from the table, I went up to retrieve my vase and look at the ones in the box that I had gotten for one dollar. There was the dark blue medium-sized vase, a pinkish red vase that was about the same size as the blue one. There were a few bud vases that only holds one or two flowers, and some more medium-sized ones that had a flower design on the front. I must write this on my bidding card, so I know how much I have spent. Oh, looks like ten dollars and fifty cents so far.

Then he moved on to the other items, and he continued selling until almost all items and boxes that were on the tables were sold. There were several boxes of couch pillows, and they all look like they were homemade. The last items on this table were the box of mismatched silverware and kitchen items and the box of cookbooks. Some people were walking away and going to the next area where things would sell. I thought to myself, "Oh good, walk away so I have a better chance of getting a good deal on the silverware box and the cookbooks." Oh, I should not say that, because the family has lost loved ones and may need the money. I speculated on how challenging it must be for them.

So first he bellowed, "How about ten dollars for this box of treasured silverware? ANYONE!" Some looked at it and walked away so I shrugged. I bid one dollar. He shouted, "ONE DOLLAR! I got one dollar do I hear two, yes! I got two dollars. Now do I hear three?" I shook my head yes at three dollars, and the lady that was bidding against me shook her head no while walking away. I then heard, "SOLD for three dollars."

Yippee! I got it. I got it! Now I had to add three dollars to my card which made it thirteen fifty. *Good! I got the silverware*, I stuttered to myself. I was full of excitement over winning the bid on the silverware. We had just a few silverwares at home, and when we were running out, I used plastic spoons and forks. Yes, I washed the plastic silverware and used them again and again. I would use them until they would crack, then throw them away.

Okay, I need to slow down on my bidding so I can bid on other things,

---

18

I told myself. There are so many unique items here that I can find in addition to the silverware. Like the cookbooks, yes, they were selling next. Oh, my I should get over there! I like buying box lots of stuff. Okay, there was a couple older ladies and a younger man wanting the cookbooks. He started them out at twenty-five dollars, "Who will give me twenty-five for this box of cookbooks? Come on, ladies, there is probably a recipe that you have been looking for in here," he openly bellowed to those listening.

One lady muttered, "How about one dollar?"

Allen kidded, "You know that there are some good recipes in here. How about five dollars? Anybody, five dollars. I got one dollar, how about two?"

So he went on with his chant.

The lady spoke loudly YES, and he went to three. Three dollars I nodded; I will give three dollars. Allen boasted, "I got three dollars now four. Four dollars now. Will anybody give four dollars?"

The lady smilingly belted, "YES!"

So he pointed to me and announced, "How about five, five dollars, I got four, now can I get five?"

I nodded, "Yes, five dollars."

"I've got five dollars, now six!" He looked at the lady that was bidding and repeated, "I got five now I need six," and she shook her head no.

Allen looked around and repeated it again. "Anybody give six dollars, I got five, now six. Six dollars anybody, going once! SOLD for five dollars!"

Oh! I got them. YES! I got them. For five dollars! Yes, five dollars. Every time I bid on something and get it, I get so giddy and proud of myself. Hope I can find some good recipes among them. I was so excited to get the cookbooks. I could not wait to look through them. Older ladies were great cooks, but most of their recipes were in their head and they would make everything from memory. You know, a dash of this and a pinch of that. Looking through the cookbooks, there were recipes written on paper along with a dusting of dried flour. I was so anxious to look through them when I got them home.

Well, there was not anything else on the other tables that interested me, so I quickly took my box of baskets, vases, silverware, and cookbooks to the car. I had to make four trips.

I added the five dollars for the cookbooks on my bidding card, and now my total is eighteen dollars and fifty cents. My, I am doing pretty good. I got all four of the things I had bid on.

I walked around and looked at stuff. I looked out over the crowd and examined the kind of people here. I did not see many teenagers here other than the Amish boys. There were several older ladies; yes, older than me. Lots of men and I noticed the different kinds of hats and some with no hat. Some with beards and some with mustache and some had stubbles that looked like they could use a shave. The men must have been there because of all the tools being sold today. I did not see many adults around my age. So women my age don't go to auctions, I guess. I was exploring the people there just to satisfy my curiosity of who and what kind of people attend auctions.

Boy, there was some genuinely nice, crocheted items in a box, along with doilies and tablecloths and other items so neatly handcrafted probably by the wife of the household. She must have been a special loving person with all the sewing she did. There were handmade quilts and bedspreads in several boxes. I love quilts and have a great appreciation for what it takes to make them. Nothing warms the home like an old-fashioned patchwork quilt.

There is something intrinsically special about that personal touch and investment. I did need a bedspread for Brian and Patty's beds, and they were not picky about what it looked like just as long as it was warm.

I could see that it would be awhile before Allen got to the quilts and comforters, so I went and stood on the back porch that was off the kitchen to get out of the hot sun. There were several empty boxes tossed in here. It looked like this was the laundry room at one time. The windows were open, so I could see and hear the auction. There were a couple ladies inside talking about the items that were selling. These ladies must have been family. There was a guy standing by the sink. Looks like they might be daughters of the deceased lady. I wondered if the guy was her son or one of these ladies' hubby.

I don't like to eavesdrop, but one lady, possibly in her mid-forties, spoke loudly and commented to the other, "Did you ever see so much junk? My gosh! They never threw anything away. And that crocheted stuff of doilies and placemats and even a big old crocheted tablecloth that Mom made, well, who used them anymore," she stammered. "Just something else to wash. Momma always wanted to give us these old things. And those quilts and hideous comforters, I would not dream of using those old things. Momma kept insisting that each of us girls should get one of those comforters that she made." The older lady, possibly in her mid-fifties replied, "Those brown comforters smell, they smell like coffee or tea. Ugg, I hate coffee! They were ugly," she uttered. "Momma kept saying they are special, and she made them especially for the two of us."

The older lady fumed, "She even put our name on them. Well, I put mine in that big box with the quilts and sheets," she blurted. The other lady replied, "I did too. I am sure some sucker can buy them because we surely don't want them."

Well, this got my curiosity up. As I was walking away, the ladies continued to chat about the items for sale. So I went out and looked in the box of blankets and quilts. Oh my, but these quilts were so pretty and well made. One was pink and white, and the other was maroon and white and looked like they each displayed a big plaid flower, the size of a sunflower, in the center. Wow, they were beautiful, so lovely, and handmade, with tiny little stitches. They should not just be thrown into a big box with other blankets and throws. Why didn't they put them in a plastic to keep them clean? I remembered an old saying I heard about old quilts, "A stitch in time saves nine." Nine stitches make an inch. Each was delicately stitched with lots of love and care. What a talented lady. Just think of the hours and days she spent making these for her daughters.

Looking on, I spotted the comforters that were just outside the back door. Two overstuffed comforters. I smelled them. Well, they vaguely smelled a little bit like coffee or was it tea? But they also smelled musty, like they had been stuffed in a box somewhere. Oh, my, there they were, two beautifully handmade comforters all tossed into these big boxes together with other stuff. I pulled out the comforters, and they were a faded, dark rusty brown at the bottom but there was a light brown above that, with a variety of plaid patchwork squares that were weaved here and there. Each square was carefully hand-stitched and some of the stitching was bigger than the other and each square was knotted at the corner with various sized squares. They looked like they were made for a single bed. They each were put together with lots and lots of stuffing which made them look thick and bulky. But it was the love that was put into them that made them special. I thought, *I wonder if Brian and Patty would use one of these on their bed? I just might bid on these.* Comforters are usually warm enough to use without a blanket underneath.

Brian's room was always cold unless he left the door open to get heat because there was no register in the floor. Brian was always cold just like me.

Typically, a comforter is defined as a thick bedding topper filled with down or a synthetic substitute. I call it stuffing. Many comforters are sewn through top to bottom or quilted to keep the filling in place, but unlike a quilt, a comforter's stitching is not ornately patterned. The amount and type of fill determined how much warmth a comforter provides. These were well stuffed and heavy.

Well, the quilts will probably sell separately because they bring a lot. In with the big box of comforters were blankets and sheets plus a box of bed pillows and pillowcases.

I walked around the tables and waited for them to sell off all the trinket items. Then they went to the lamps and then the box of doilies. The lovely doilies. Oh my, I wonder what these would bring. I remembered there were some beautiful pieces in there. I should not bid on them because I wanted to have enough money for the comforters. They were bidding them up high, so I walked away as they were selling for twenty-five dollars and more. After they sold, I walked over to the lady that bought them and told her how beautiful they were and how I had admired them. She seemed like a nice warmhearted lady.

With a gleam in her eyes, she said, "I will use them to make barbie doll dresses for my grandchildren." With a smile on my face, I told her that was so nice of her and how lovely I thought they were. Those beautiful doilies would make some lovely doll dresses. This reminded me of my grandma Price because she crocheted a lot of doilies and tablecloths along with Afghans and winter scarfs. She is the one that taught me to crochet.

The afternoon sunbathed the items on the tables as the warm rays of sunshine spread across the backyard. I remembered and as I had seen before that it's not unheard of for unscrupulous bidders to switch the contents from box to box. I just witnessed it here in front of me.

They were getting close to the end of things on and around the tables and now it was the box of sheets, quilts, blankets, and comforters up next. They held up the two quilts which were just beautiful with such dainty little stitches in each design and lots of people bid on them, and they finally sold for one hundred and seventy-five dollars each and the person bought both.

I looked around and Brian was not around. I thought about asking him if he liked the comforter for his bed. Next up were the comforters. I was beginning to feel excited and a little exhilarated again. They were not as pretty as the quilts, and the colors were not as vibrant but a little faded; however, the attention that was given to the stitching was miraculous. Okay, here we go on the bidding. He asked for twenty-five dollars for each one, then for both. No one would open the bid. I waited to see if they would go any lower, and they did because no one was bidding on them. Bud held them up with the help of Allen.

I held up my hand and blurted, "I will give five dollars for each of the comforters."

"I got five, now SIX!" he yelled. "Anyone want to give six dollars, six dollars anyone! I've got five dollars, now do I hear six, six, six. Six dollars anyone? I heard that it is going to get mighty cold this winter," he joked. Some of them laughed but no one would bid on them. Immediately I heard "SOLD!"

Oh, oh, oh, I got them! Just like that! You would have thought I had won a treasure chest. He asked, "Do you want them both?" and I shouted yes! At least I thought I did. I just love it when a plan comes together. *Thank you, Lord,* I chanted to myself. I took the comforters and laid them on one of the empty tables.

Moving on, one lady told me she wanted the rest of the box of blankets, so she was waiting for the quilts and comforters to sell. Now that they had sold, they were to auction off the box of blankets and sheets and pillowcases. I waited around to see what they would sell for and who got them. I commented to her that the blankets were nice, and the sheets looked like they were for a queen bed and that there were some pillowcases in there. Again, no one was interested in them.

The lady chimed in, "I will give five dollars for them."

"So I heard five dollars, I got five dollars, do I hear six? Now who will give me six, six dollars anyone?" They sold for five dollars each, for the two boxes. I believe there were four blankets and several sheets and pillowcases in the boxes. The excitement of winning ran through my whole body. I was so excited that I had gotten the comforters, and I don't think those ladies in the house that were complaining appreciated anything their mother made them. These patchwork comforters were knotted here and there, and the stitching was all done by hand. There were several unique pieces of scrap material that made up this comforter. There was an abundance of stuffing and batting in them that probably made them heavy. I found a big garbage bag on the back porch and stuffed them down in it.

As I was walking away, the lady that bought the blankets and sheets hollered at me, "Honey," she pointed to me and smiled, "I found some pillow shams that match your comforters down in the bottom of my box. There were four of them."

I spoke, "Oh MY! They do match! Thank you so much for finding them. Can I buy them from you?"

She responded, "No, you can have them, dear," and she piled them into my arms.

I smiled and insisted, "No, I want to pay you for them." I reached in my pocket and held out a five-dollar bill. "Here, how about five dollars for all of them?"

She stuttered, Oh honey, you don't have to do that."

I replied, "You paid for them, so I want you to have some money for them. Here, this should cover it. Five dollars for the two set of shams."

She was delighted to get the money and grinned, "Thank you, dear," as she walked away, I returned a thank you for offering them. I stuffed them down into the bag with the comforters. They had the patchwork pattern on them with the brown faded ruffle just like the comforters.

I made sure I wrote the comforters down on my bidding card for ten dollars. I thought to myself, *Boy, I am doing good.* I was looking at my bidding card and thought, *I am not over my budget yet and just look at all the neat stuff I have bought. So many treasures,* at least they were treasures to me.

They were done with the household items and next up was the farm items. However, the farm items were not going to sell till one o'clock. Well, that would be in fifteen minutes.

The blazing midday sun shone relentlessly on the bidders. I loaded up the comforters that I had purchased and put them in the car.

The farmers and other men were all gathered around the farm tractors and wagons, awaiting the start of the tools and farm stuff that would sell. The gray tractor, I believe this is a Ford tractor, was in good condition. There was a reddish-orange one, I believe this is a Farmall and it is a tricycle type, but it was faded a lot with some rust here and there.

Then I went over close to where Carl was, and he was close to the rototiller. He was leaning up against a small building that looked like a tool shed. I waited to see what it would sell for and talked to

Carl about my purchases, and he was waiting to buy some tools. He commented, Brian does a good job with helping Allen out with the auctions. Oh yes, he really enjoys doing that and he likes to help Allen with his auctions.

There were hammers, saws, screwdrivers and wrenches, tape measures by the dozens, flashlights of various sizes, boxes of nails and screws, shovels, pitch forks, hay hooks, tool-boxes full of tools, wooden boxes full of tools and nails by the boxes and so much other stuff. I was not sure what some of them were, but they looked like antique tools, if that's what you call them. There was even box lots of tools and lighting equipment and buckets full of stuff. This must have been a collection of tools spanning fifty to sixty years. These were all piled on top and around the wagons, big hay wagons. I spotted a small collection of chain saws of various sizes.

I told Carl, "I should buy me a little chain saw. I might need one sometime."

He cautiously replied, "No, you don't need a chain saw because you might saw your leg off. If you need something sawed up, call me and I will come over and take care of it." I let out a big sigh, rolled my eyes at him, and mumbled okay.

As luck would have it, they sold all the tools before selling the tiller. After about an hour, they got over to it. They started the tiller out at five hundred dollars. Oh no! I cannot afford anything close to that. Then I heard two hundred, then one hundred, I got one hundred now how about one fifty, YES he shouted. I got one fifty, then one sixty and then he shouted, "I got one sixty and now I need one seventy, yes, one seventy anyone?" No one else bid so I heard, "Sold for one sixty." Darn, I should have known it would go high. Oh well, guess I will be tilling up my flower beds and garden by shovel, one shovel at a time.

I told Carl, "I am not interested in any tools, so I think I will go home."

I had been there six hours no seven hours. Oh, what an enjoyable seven hours of excitement, enjoying the expressions on the high bidder's face as they won the bid. The look of folks and their anticipation of what might be up next for them to bid on.

I headed over to where Lynn was taking the money, and I spotted a green old, faded round plastic picnic table beside the wagons. There were no chairs to it, but it did have an umbrella with it, but it too was faded by time. It had a collection of canning jars and canning supplies stacked on it. I hung around a little longer just to see what it would sell for. I talked to Lynn awhile since no one was checking out yet.

I asked Lynn, "Who got number one today? You know, the one Mom always gets when I bring her."

Lynn exclaimed, "No one gets that number. We start out with number 2 because that will always be Ma's number and no one else."

I felt a little twinkle or a flutter in my heart after she remarked. My throat got a little lump in it as I tried to tell Lynn, "Oh, Leigh and Mom were going shopping today for all of the August birthdays. She would have been so overjoyed that you had done that, Lynn. She likes to come to the auctions. Mom likes to bid on the box-lot items too, just to see all the special things that are in there. I am sure she comes also to hear Allen shout out his chant because she is so proud of him. You could see it in her eyes." *Boy she would love to see what was in that box of silverware and cookbooks*, I thought.

I told Lynn, "You know, it turned out to be a beautiful day," and she agreed.

Looking out toward the barn, the tool auction had started, and I could see three or four wagons with some tools on top and gas cans and wheel rims under the wagons, tires, and ropes all neatly laid out.

Allen was getting close to the table and canning stuff. I wondered why these were not sold with the dishes and stuff on the tables. There were lots of boxes of mason jars, several boxes of lids and rings for the jars, all laid out on the table that I wanted. I did see several crocks on the wagon, but they were already sold. Now how did I miss them? There were three folding chairs that sold for just three dollars. The Amish guys bought up all the boxes of mason jars, lids, and rings. There were some cast-iron items of pots and skillets and platters. Coal buckets and shovels on the wagons. The Amish were bidding on these items also.

Wow! That coal bucket brought back some memories of shoveling ashes out of the stoves when I was growing up at home. That was a nasty job.

When all the items on the picnic table were sold, he started auctioning off the dark-green faded picnic table. So no one would bid on it as he started it out with ten dollars, then five dollars, then I held up my hand and bid one dollar.

"Do I hear two dollars?" he mused. "Two dollars anyone?" Then I heard SOLD! OMG! I got it for just one dollar. I felt that tug and warm feeling of excitement again. Yes, that giddy feeling. I felt proud of myself that I got it for just one dollar. I looked it over and thought that it would be a nice table to use when transplanting my flowers. Now, oh no, I noticed that it does not come apart or fold up or anything, how will I get it home in my car? I am driving a small, old woman's car, as Brian calls it. It is a Ford Tempo, and it is an '80s something. Ahh, I think it is an '85. I should have thought about this sooner. Oh dear! What to do?

I spotted Carl still there, so I went over and asked him, "Can you drop off a picnic table at my house on your way home since you have a truck?" He was fine with that, so I loaded the table onto his truck. I didn't ask Brian because he did not have a tailgate on his truck.

He asked, "Why did you buy that ugly thing? It is faded so much."

I added, "I plan to paint it and bring back its beauty. It looks sturdy and made of some kind of hard plastic." He responded okay, after rolling his eyes at me.

I bought me a shredded chicken sandwich and then went to pay for my purchases. Then I heard on the loud announcement.

"WOULD THE OWNER OF A BROWN FORD TEMPO MOVE YOUR CAR? LICENSE PLATE NUMBER PRM1931. YOU ARE BLOCKING THE SALE OF AN ITEM."

I thought . . . Brown Ford Tempo? SALE! Oh! Oh! that is ME! OH NO! They can't sell my car, I chanted to myself. I figured, since I found a good spot, I would get in trouble for it. I hurriedly went over to my car and moved it. OMG! There is this old rusty plow or disc, or some sort of machinery stowed in a bunch of weeds. Okay, I drove around behind the barn and found an open spot in the second row. It was a fer piece . . . as the ole timers say. So I walked back up to the trailer to pay for my treasures.

I felt quite proud of what I bought. As I was paying for my purchases, I told Lynn that I was happy to get the comforters and how proud I was to get them for five dollars each. I told her about the baskets, and I liked the picnic basket that I bought. I felt like going in and telling the ladies in the house that I bought the ugly comforters, so they will not have to worry about them, but I did not. I paid for my purchases which totaled twenty-nine dollars and fifty cents. I should add the five dollars I paid for the shams. Gosh, I have some money left over. This is fine and dandy. I just love it when a plan comes together. Thank you, Lord Jesus, for giving me this beautiful day and allowing me to mingle with all the bidders. Even though I do not know them, this is something that we all like to do so there is a bonding of some sort.

I surreptitiously slipped away and walked to my car. Although there were still many cars still there, I had seen all the items that I was interested in buying. On my drive home, I kept thinking of the things I got, all the baskets and box-lot items. Boy, Mom would like to go through the box lots with me. We can find beauty in all the little things that matter to us, reminding ourselves of the moments that inspired us, big or small, the inspiration provides us with a purpose and gratitude.

The gentle breeze had picked up some, cooling the afternoon air and in all the pleasures of such a beautiful and prosperous day. The road to life has many twists and turns and no two directions seem to be the same. Yet our lessons come from the journey that we experienced and not the destination we encountered. We couldn't be the person we are today without those yesterdays. So, I can dream big and keep my worries small. Your future is yours to own so make every moment count and make it a special part of your memory.

Sometimes life goes on in peaceful cycles like the seasons, a gradual blending of time and events that were scarcely noticed or remembered. I will remember this auction for a few years to come and treasure the items that I have purchased.

My adventure for today had come to an end and I will unpack all the treasures, but my memory of all the people there will fade into my past with the exception of my family members that were there.

CHAPTER 2

Unpacking the Treasures

When I got home that afternoon, my daughter Patty had the radio blaring in her room. She had her room cleaned up some. It was a small room and she had one single bed that was once a bunk bed, a desk and a chest of drawers. I showed her the comforters. She hugged them and joked, "They were heavy but smelled like coffee." She wanted to try it on her bed, but I told her I wanted to wash them first.

I asked her, "Patty, what do you think of the comforter and the shams?"

She replied, "They are all right, but not that pretty because it was faded some, but it would keep me warm."

I told her, "I only paid five bucks for it." It has pillow shams too!

She remarked, "They looked like something you would find in a log cabin."

I replied, "I will remember that when I get my log cabin. It is nice and kind of bulky and heavy, so I believe it should be warm," I told her.

After church the next day, I had to wash one comforter at a time since they were quite bulky, and all I had was a stackable washer with a dryer on top. It took a while, but I got them washed and hung them out onto the clothesline to dry along with the shams. The washing had faded them out a little bit. They still had a vague smell of coffee or tea. I think I know what I am smelling. To get the antique or brown look to the comforters, I believe she soaked the material in coffee or tea to give them the old-fashion look. I have heard or read that this gives the article that old time antique look. However, the recipe says that if you rinse the article in vinegar, it is supposed to set the color and take the coffee smell away. If that is the case, you would think the coffee smell would be gone by now. I put some vinegar in the washing machine when I washed them. With the comforters out onto the clothesline in the backyard, I was hoping the sunshine beaming down on them, would get rid of the coffee smell and it won't take long for them to dry.

That afternoon, I brought them inside and they smelled fresh from the sunshine and did not smell of any coffee or tea. I helped Patty put one on her bed. Since she had a bunk bed, it was long and hung over the side of her bed, almost to the floor. That's good, it will hide all the junk she keeps under her bed.

I put Brian's on his bed, and it too hung over a lot. I put the pillow sham on one of their pillows. I will have to buy them each another pillow to put the other sham on their bed. They did not look to bad, they were clean, and they would keep them warm. They had that nice country look. Even though I added vinegar to the wash and fabric softener to the rinse, Patty smirked; they still vaguely smelled like coffee. Well, Patty liked coffee, but Brian did not. I told her, "I do not smell the coffee now that I washed them. I only smell the sunshine and the fabric softener."

I rummaged through the box of vases and was pleased with them because I knew I could use them sometime. I thought the dark blue one and the deep pink colored one was pretty. I set the big vase in the basement on a shelf along with the box of vases. I kept thinking of what all I could do with this big vase. I could use it for long-stemmed flowers, but I thought also I could put in branches of my rose bushes with the leaves still on it. This would give the arrangement that natural touch of a more modern décor.

I showed Patty the box of silverware as I was taking it out of the trunk and placed it onto the back patio and sat it on my round table that once was used to wrap electrical wire around. I got it from a jobsite that Carl was working on. Speaking of Carl, he had left the table sometime yesterday.

Patty started rummaging through the box with me. I told her that there is something black in that box that will get on your hands. "I think it is coal dust or ashes." She proceeded to take the items out of the box one by one. She made several piles of the various patterns of silverware. We did find a matched set of service for six silverwares. They were silver with black plastic on the handle. I got a big pan and put them in it and added some baking soda and vinegar to the water and boiled them. Hopefully, this will kill all the germs. After they boiled for a while, I rinsed them off and soaked them in warm water for a little bit and then added dish soap and washed and dried them off.

She kept looking at the kitchen items and came across a round green plastic thing with a smaller hole in the center.

She asked, "Mom, this thing looks strange. Do you know what it is?"

I looked at it and examined it. It had "Gourmet Specialties" on the handle. "I believe this is an egg separator," I told her. "When you only want the whites of an egg and not the yolk or vice-versa. You use it when you are making a meringue for a pie or some kinds of candy."

She quizzically remarked, "Okay, I never saw anything like this. This might be handy to have some day," and she put it aside.

She kept looking at all the different kitchen stuff. She found a hand can opener that you cranked, and I had to tell her what it was for and showed her how to use it. Then she found another opener. It was used to open cans of cream so you can pour the content out. It was also used to open bottles, like pop bottles before there was the twist off that we have today, and you can also open the flats on canning jars, like green beans and stuff. There were a couple pocketknives and one of them had Elvis on it. Oh gosh! I did get something with Elvis. I washed it off and set it out on the patio table to dry and added it to my Elvis memorabilia.

As I was digging through the box of silverware, there were three small Bic lighters, two sets of aluminum measuring spoons, pie servers, two potato mashers, a pastry blender, nut crackers, butter knives, various unmatched coasters and there was a key opener that was used to open coffee cans, a few years ago, and a few small strainers. I added the items that needed sterilized to my pan to add baking soda and vinegar and we found several partial sets of silverware. I can donate them to the Good Will or have a yard sale. I have heard that campers use mismatched items for camping trips.

There were some unique items in the bottom of the box. Patty started shuffling through the coal dust and she grinned, "Look, I found an old coin." She held it up with her blackened fingers and said, "It looks old and has a man on it. They probably do not make these anymore, do they, Mom?"

I replied, "Oh! It is a silver dollar. Oh, look how tarnished and very worn out it is. It had Liberty on it and was dated 1941." I took it and smiled, "Oh, this is old," I giggled. "See if there are any more."

We both took turns digging, and we found some more coins of buffalo nickels and some pennies. I told her, "I will wash them up and we can read the date better. We will keep these and put them in safekeeping. I will have to check with Uncle Allen to see if they are worth anything. He collects old coins and knows a lot about them."

She and I both kept looking in the box and we had found six silver dollars, five buffalo nickels, and fifteen pennies in the bottom of the silverware tray. One of the silver dollars had Eisenhower on one side and the Liberty bell on the other side.

Among the black coal dust, I also found four Kennedy half dollars and told Patty that these are old and may be worth something. She had a gleam in her eye as if she had just won a jackpot and said, are they worth more than fifty cents?

They must have not known they were in there. That took care of one tray of silverware and things. All of them were tarnished with age, and some even had dried dirt on them. Let me put them in some water and clean them up a little bit.

So I put the coins into the baking soda and vinegar water, while Patty continued to search the next silverware tray. There was lots of unmatched silverware. There was a box of flats for large-mouthed canning jars, cookie cutters, dippers, and food thermometers. I wonder if they still work, I told Patty.

Hopefully, this solution will take the tarnish off the coins. After I let them soak in the baking soda for a while, I put them into a hot-water-and-dish-soap bath and made some soapy water to clean them up. Wow, they cleaned up nicely, and there was enough silverware for at least eight people. The nickels and pennies and half dollars came clean and so did the silver dollars.

Patty was fascinated as she continued to rummage through the box and finding numerous old knives and jar openers. There were ladles, pie servers, and numerous tablespoons of various sizes, some iced teaspoons and measuring spoons of various sizes, several paring knives. There was one knife she did not know what it was for, so she described it to me by yelling the description to me from the porch to inside the house.

She hollered, "MOM, I found this one knife and it looks a lot different than a table knife, it is fat at the top and smaller on the handle." She held it up as I looked through the back door.

I replied, "Oh! That is a butter knife. Yes, at some fancy dinners, you put a butter knife in the butter. That was before they had soft butter."

Patty responded, "Well, there are six of them, and they all look alike. They must have had big parties if each butter dish had a knife." She jokingly responded, "MOM! Will you have a dinner party so we can use butter knives? I think they are neat." She laughed, "Huh! A knife just for butter."

We both continued to sort through the powdery coal dust and found a bunch of little forks and spoons. I told Patty that I thought these were used with caviar, which is a delicacy among the rich and famous. She asked, "Caviar, what is that now?"

Laughingly I told her, "They are fish eggs."

She responded with "Yuck! Ewe! Don't think I want to eat those. But the forks and spoons are cute, Mom," she shouted as she was holding them up. They too were covered with coal dust so she tossed them into the pan of water. There wasn't much left in the box but coal dust, so I told her to go dump it in the corner of the driveway. When she dumped it, she found some more pennies and nickels.

We both had the coal dust on our fingers, and they even smelled like coal. We washed them in the dish soap, and it all came off okay. It was fun to see all the old kitchen items that were not used anymore. I replaced the water several times and got all the items sterilized and washed up. I left the strainers out on the table in the sunshine to dry.

We gathered up all the clean items and took them in the house. I had to find a place for them in my silverware drawer and the other trinkets I took down in the basement and put into a plastic tub. I gladly tossed out the plastic silverware that I had accumulated.

When Brian came home, he found the comforter on his bed. He asked, "Who put that blanket on my bed?"

I answered, "I did. It was one of the treasures that I got at Allen's auction. It is washed and dried and smells like sunshine," I told him.

He boasted, "It looks warm, but it looks like something the Amish would make." He gave me a little hug and added, "Thanks a lot for the comforter, mom, and thanks for cleaning up my room."

I confessed, "I did not do the cleaning part. Patty did that after she had run the sweeper in her room, she run it in your room."

Then she joked, "Okay, brother, you owe me big time!"

I was proud of all the unique things I found at the auction. The coins were incredibly old, and I wonder if they are collector's items. I was glad the silverware turned out okay and the tarnish came off them and all the other things. They looked new. The cake and pie servers turned out great! Each had a different design on the handles and there were six of them. One of the cake knives and server had a clear handle and the server part came out clear, so clear you could see yourself in it. I wondered if this was used in a wedding.

I took all the baskets out of the big box and lined them up on the patio. Using the garden hose, I sprayed them good to get all the cobwebs and other debris off of them. I let them dry in the cool evening air as the light breeze was cooling the evening down.

The three holiday tins that were with the baskets all had Christmas designs on them. They were pretty and had some colorful designs of the holiday.

One was a rectangle Holiday tin with a Christmas village and a horse pulling a snow sled carriage. It was around four inches deep. I opened it up and found it full of beautiful colors of ribbons. These were ribbons you might put around a doily or you could put them in someone's hair, like in a ponytail. There were many pretty bright colors. I guess Patty was too old for me to put ribbons in her hair. However, I do remember putting ribbons in her long red hair and that was when she was maybe four or five years old.

There was one that was square with a Santa's workshop scene on it. It also was around four inches deep. Inside, it contained numerous spools of various colors of thread. This will be handy to use in my sewing machine. Unless it is so brittle, I may have to just use it in a needle when I need to sew something. Yes, it does break apart easy.

Next was the red one which was round with a Christmas candle in the center. It was only about three inches deep. It contained buttons. Lots and lots of buttons. I remember my grandma Price had tins of buttons. She would give us the job of finding matching buttons and using large safety pins; we would put all the matching buttons on a safety pin. This kept us busy for a few hours.

The picnic basket was neat looking, with two lids attached to a piece of round wood going across the middle of the basket that connected to the handle. Each lid would open to reveal the content. I took the liner off and washed it. I have never seen one made quite like this one. Most of the baskets had handles on them, except for the flat one. Looked like it could be used as a basket you would put a hot casserole dish on.

It was fun going through the boxes of various items. I am sure I will get as much enjoyment from them as the previous owner did.

I decided to go through the cookbooks at a later time since it was getting time for me to fix some supper. So I left them in the trunk of my car until I was ready to go through them.

Raising the two kids hadn't been easy but it was important to me to know that I was doing the best I could at the time I was doing it, even if my best sometimes wasn't all that good. I believe that your children are a reflection of who you are and how well I did with raising them. There are many responsibilities to parenting and I had to be both father and mother to them. I wanted to make sure I had done all that I could to give them the basic things they needed in life and the spirit and enthusiasm to live with passion and experience the joy in what life had to offer them.

Chapter 3

The Cookbooks

It was a beautiful Sunday morning and a perfect opportunity to thank God for reminding me how blessed I am. The faint chirping of the robins, blue jays, and sparrows were added to my awakening sounds as the golden rays of the morning sun shone down on me. I watched as a squirrel scurried around the yard. He had bulging cheeks, so he must have something in his mouth. I was enjoying my morning cup of coffee out on the patio as I was remembering all the neat things I got at the auction. They were neat to me but was probably junk to some. I heard the faint whistle of the train off, way off in a distance. I wondered as it was going through Raymond, was it headed to Marysville or going the other way. I was subconsciously thinking of what it would be like to travel on a train. However, it would have to be a passenger train and not a freight train. I could feel the swaying, back and forth, back and forth. I was awakened from my daydream when Patty came out onto the porch and asked if I was going to church today.

I answered, "Well, I sure am. Are you going with me?" She hesitated a few minutes and then replied, "Yes, I believe I will go with you. I will call my friend and see if she is going. Can we sit together if she comes?"

"I don't care if you do," I replied. She went in and called her friend.

Oh! Patty Jo! I yawned. She had joined me on the patio and stretched herself on one of the chairs. "It sure is going to be a beautiful day today. I can just feel it in the air and in my bones. So did you like covering up with the blanket or should I say comforter?"

She gaspingly stated, "No, it been was too hot in my room. I slept with the fan on all night. Actually, Mom," she hesitantly replied, "I have been laying on top of it. It was not too bad, and it had good packing but in some places it was hard."

Unfortunately, we did not have air conditioning in the house or ceiling fans at the time.

"Well, I am glad you slept well, and I plan to go through the cookbooks this afternoon after church."

I was done with my coffee, so I headed in to get my second cup and a yogurt. I asked Patty, "So is there anything I can get you for breakfast? I got yogurt and doughnuts. Do you want any?"

"Oh," she yawned, and shouted, "I will take one of each. Can I have a cup of coffee too?"

I let her drink coffee once in a while. I got me a tray, which was bought at an auction, and made us each a cup of coffee by warming the water in the microwave and took two yogurts and doughnuts outside and put the tray on the table. I put the cream and sugar in both coffees because she likes it the same way I do. We sat and chatted about school as we enjoyed our breakfast outside on the deck. A flood of childhood memories surfaced as we both reminisced about the days gone by.

It was important for my kids to know that I would always be there for them. I will always see them through any choices they make in life. As the years go by, I feel that despite some difficult times along the way, I have absolutely, positively got to be one of the most blessed mothers in the world. I chose the word blessed, rather than lucky, because I believe that God has personally watched over me and my family, every step of the way and each and every day.

Patty carried the tray inside, and we both got ready for church. Brian woke up and ate his breakfast by himself in the kitchen. He did not like coffee, so he drank a big glass of milk and some doughnuts. The biggest glass he could find in the cupboard. Brian did not go to church since he was older now. He and I talked about this and decided that he would go when he was ready. No sense forcing him to go if he is not ready. That would be defeating the purpose for going.

At church, I told Leigh about all the treasures that I had gotten at the auction. Patty told her about the silver dollars that we had found in the box of silverware. Leigh told us about the gifts she and Mom got for everybody that had birthdays in August. However, she didn't mention what she bought Patty since her birthday is in August. Mother could not hear me well enough when I told her and Leigh what I got at the auction. I did not want to yell it out in church so I told her I will tell you later. Patty and her friend sat one row behind us and chatted and giggled on occasion.

When we got home, we looked around the house and Brian was nowhere to be found. He is not too good about telling me where he is going. So I fixed dinner for Patty and me, which was spaghetti and meatballs, with garlic bread and a small salad, and we had some warm applesauce. After we ate, I cleaned up the table and put the dishes in the sink. I had no dishwasher here, of course, so we did dishes, the old-fashion way, by hand. I washed them, and Patty dried them. After dinner, Patty went over to the ballpark and met up with some of her friends to play ball.

I called Mother to see if she wanted to come over and rummage through the cookbooks with me. She said she had company at the time but said she would like to go through and read some of the recipes sometime. I told her I would bring them over to her, and she could read some of them.

I backed my car down the grass-covered driveway up to the patio. As I was taking the box of cookbooks out of the car, I placed them on the round green table that I bought at the auction yesterday. Yes, it is here. Carl must have just dropped it off and then left. I do not know when he brought it. I just found it on the patio the next morning. I sat down in the patio chair and took out one of the cookbooks and laid it on the table and briefly thumbed through it. It had some paper cutouts of recipes stuck into some of the pages.

Some of my fondest memories take me back to mealtimes with my big family. All ten or eleven of us sometimes all gathered around this long table. Some on chairs and some on the long bench. Yes, it was crowded with eight of nine kids at a table, and always one in a high chair. The aroma of the food that Mom prepared looked delicious and as the meal was passed around, you knew you had better get what you wanted the first time because there were seldom seconds left. I do not know how she did it, cooking for that many. We grew up eating what she liked to cook and never thought to find that there were other foods that mom didn't like that were good also. That was until we got out on our own and experimented with other foods.

I am so blessed to have inherited some of Mother's skills and the love of preparing the awesome meals. She taught us at an early age the basics of cooking. I recall an old saying, "I have been cooking since I was 'knee high to a grasshopper.'" One thing Mother always did, and

I thought was unnecessary, was everything she fixed on the stove, and it was an old cook stove by the way, she cooked in a pan or a cast-iron skillet. Then when we were ready to eat, she would put the food in a bowl or on a plate to be passed around the table. So many dishes were dirtied and lots and lots of dishes to wash, by hand, of course.

As years went by, my cooking skills expanded to new dimensions—from southern or country cooking to some more elegant dishes. And I do not put the food into dishes very much anymore. I think the food will stay hot if you leave it on the stove and fill your plate. Maybe Mother thought we might spill our plate on the floor.

While middle-age years came about, even before my "middle-age spread" expanded me, my "Dessert Queen" title was forfeited to healthier meals with desserts becoming a rare delicacy. Somehow, I learned to bake and decorate cakes for special occasions. This work fascinated and thrilled me as the ingredients I blend usually transpires into delectable dishes. Just remember, the main ingredient in preparation of a dish is love.

Most of the ingredients listed in the old cookbooks were staples before processed foods became commonplace in the grocery stores. Many of the recipes found there came from that era where it was all "cooking from scratch." Just a few simple ingredients were the norm.

Some of the pages of the cookbooks were yellowed, stained, and scribbled in with some torn pages, but some were pretty much perfect. There were cookbooks back to 1955 with some hardback and some just paperbacked; anyway, I enjoyed thumbing through them and the treasures that they held within them.

There was a total of ten cookbooks of various sizes and thickness. I took each one out of the box and quickly examined them as I stacked them on the table one by one. Some were in bad shape and others had the remains of butter and flour dried on them. I believe the American Home cookbook had the kind of foods that my family would like; however, it was missing the front and back cover.

The next cookbook was *Cooking with Jean* and was dated 1966 and *Bread Making Made Easy* was dated 1960. I do not think I will be making my own bread. I do not eat much bread nowadays. Next was the *Cooking with Horse and Buggy People* looked like it was from the Amish because some of the recipes have lard in them. A few of the books were from local churches like *Treasured Recipes of Camp Christian and Sharing our Favorites* and the *Church of Christ Recipes*. These were spiral-bound with the plastic curlicue binding it together. There were some *Taste of Home Magazines* dated 2004 to 2006. This is a monthly magazine and I think it is still in production. The *Farmhouse Kitchen, Becky's Favorite Recipes* had several recipes that you cook in a cast-iron skillet. It was dated 1979. One cookbook was *Cooking with Foil* and was all about preparing meals in aluminum foil. Well, there you go! Would not be much cleanup if you used foil. As I flipped through the books, occasionally a written recipe would fall out or a clipping from the newspaper or magazine might be wrinkled and faded. However, if you look at the dates on them you will see how long they have been protected in their little vault. I guess, as the old saying goes, the more stains there are on the recipe, the more food was enjoyed. Now I had some idea of what kind of cookbooks were in the box. There were a couple more things in the box, but I was interrupted.

Patty had come home from the park and was thirsty and hungry. She asked, "What is there to eat? I am starving!"

I answered, "Well, what can you fix that sounds good?"

Of course, she answered, "What you got?"

I responded, "How about some corn dogs and chips. There is some Kool-Aid in the fridge." She fixed her a corn dog in the microwave and opened a bag of chips. She thought that may tie her over till I fixed supper.

She sat down at the table and asked me, "So! What is in the cookbooks?"

I told her, "Recipes!"

She laughingly answered, "DUH! MOM! Are there some good recipes in them?"

I smirked, "There might be something in here that you like." I told Patty that all these cookbooks sure make me want to try new recipes. I want to examine each one of them as I go through them. I commented to her, "This box is bursting with recipes and some that were created before microwave ovens and food processors."

Patty had decided to stretch out on the lounge chair that I use for sunbathing so I can get a tan. Let's see how long it takes for her to fall asleep.

While sorting through the first cookbook, the one with no front or back cover, I found clippings of recipes left in the pages. As I looked at the recipes in the book, I found a post card from someplace in San Francisco, California, which had a beach scene on it. It was yellowed with age. Someone by the name of Katherine had sent it to her mom and told her about a nice guy she met and was getting engaged. She signed it "Love and Kisses." I could see a postage stamped date on it, July 16, but the year was covered up with a grease spot and flour. I tried picking it off and the year came off with it.

So going on through the cookbook, I found this yellow envelope with oils and flour dried on it. It was almost the size of the American Home cookbook and was stuck into the back pages of it. It had a Velcro closure on it. There were a few written recipes stuck on it and there was a name "Katherine" something written in pencil, on the front, but it was all faded and you could barely make out what was written because of all the dried flour and oil or butter mixed with dirt and who knows what else. I carefully opened the flap on the envelope, being careful not to tear the delicate contents. I pulled out all the papers and started to examine each one of them. One looked like a grade card with handwritten letters in small boxes on the cardboard. The name on it was Katherine Moore and a date of May 7,1953. It had a place for age and grade, but it was faded so much you could not read it. It was from the Richwood school. So this was Katherine's grade card. It had all 'A's' on it.

Then I pulled out a paper wrapped in plastic wrap of some kind, or was it Saran wrap? There was a paper folded in half with a bluish-pinkish background. I thought to myself, *This must be another grade card, or could it be her diploma?* As I opened it up, I could see a ribbon at the bottom. Omg! Out fell four fifty-dollar bills. "OH! WOW!" I shouted. I laid the money off to the side and as I read on, I could see that it looked like a baptismal certificate for Katherine Moore. It was from a Church of Christ. It was yellowed a little with age. It had the Church of Christ recognition of being baptized. As I opened the next one, it was for Madalyn Moore. It was just like Katherine's. As I opened it up, laying on top was four fifty-dollar bills. Both certificates were dated Augusts 10, 1959. Yes, this were Katherine and Madalyn Moore's baptismal certificates. But what was the cash for, I questioned. I just don't understand why someone would leave cash in a baptismal certificate. And I wondered if it had been there since 1959. What a mystery, or should I say unsolvable mystery because their mother was the only one that knew these were in this envelope.

So do I keep the cash? What else can I do with it? No one knew it was there except God and the mother. Oh my, well, I knew that I should not hold my breath because things like this never happens in my favor. I will put the cash in with the coins and ask Allen about them. I looked through more papers and there were more grade cards, a birthday card that had a one on it, but this one had the name Madalyn on it. There is no rhyme or reason why these items were in this envelope that was stashed in these cookbooks.

I sorted through some more of the papers and found what looked like a marriage certificate. Yes, that is what it is, a "Certificate of Marriage." It had a name on it of Jedediah and Margarette Moore. However, this is just a certificate from the church with the date and place that they were married. It was dated August 19, 1923. Oh, my goodness, this is old. Well, it is as old as my mother. She was born in that year. I laid it in my pile of papers and went on to the next mystery.

As I continued, I also found two birth announcements. They were not the actual birth certificates but were just birth announcements. They each had baby pictures attached to each announcement on one side and a one-hundred-dollar bill on the other side. Oh gosh! THE MONEY IS REAL. They were all paperclipped together. There was a name on them, looked like it was Katherine, and the other was Madalyn. You could not read either of them very well because they were so faded. One had a date of May 7, 1947, so this one was Katherine; and the other one had September 21, 1951, and this one was Madalyn. They were a little bit yellowed with age but in good condition other than the fading. I also wondered why a one-hundred-dollar bill was attached to each announcement. I thought to myself, *Do you suppose she forgot that these were stuck in this cookbook?* Now what do I do with them, so I added it to the stack of papers and put the cash in the pile to ask Allen. I carefully put all the papers back into the envelope and laid them aside. This was my mystery envelope.

I continued to search through the rest of the cookbooks. In the next one, the *Cooking with Jean*, which was cooking with barbeque. There were also some recipes about hot potato salad. Now that was unusual. There was this long faded white envelope that was sealed. Oh, now what could this be since it was never opened. On the outside it had the name Katherine and Madalyn Watterson Moore. Should I open it or not. Well, this stuff is mine, so I carefully opened the envelope. Inside, there were two white cardboard pamphlets that looked like cards with papers inside of it, and they were all folded in thirds. As I opened each side very carefully, it revealed a certificate. On top of the award was two fifty-dollar bills. As I read through it, there was written in bold and scripted print, "The State of Ohio" I read on. Awards of two minor children, Katherine and Madalyn Watterson, to Jedediah and Margarette Moore to give full custody of these children by adoption on this day of January 19, 1953. It went on with other legal stuff. Let's see, it was from the Union County courthouse. Mother was Carol Lynn Watterson. Oh my GOSH! Those ladies at the auction were adopted! I wondered if they knew.

Immediately, I called out to Patty, "Look, look here, these are adoption certificates for those ladies at the auction. They were family members of the estate."

Patty mumbled, "What ladies?" She had dozed off as she lay in the warm sunshine.

"Oh, I responded, there was these two ladies at the auction that commented on your comforters and complained that they were ugly and couldn't wait to get them sold. Wow! What should I do with this? They must know about it, that they were adopted. I will check with Lynn as what to do with them. I recalled a show on television where people that were adopted as a child go looking for their real parents. Now, how will they know if I have the papers. Well, there might be something on file at the courthouse."

There were a few handwritten recipes in the cookbook, plus a receipt for some seed corn and soybeans. I added them to the pile and went to the next cookbook, *Bread Making Made Easy*. It was nice and had a lot of pictures in it. Lots of recipes for bread and doughnuts. I found a banana bread that was quite similar to my recipe. As I was shuffling through it, stuffed in the back was a couple books of S&H Green Stamps. I remember collecting these and TV stamps. You got stamps from grocery stores when you made your purchases and then licked them and put them into a book. You saved the books and looked in a catalogue where you could buy stuff like furniture and things for your home. I remember that I bought Brian's baby bed with Green Stamps. I shouted to Patty, "They don't make these anymore." She waved at me because she was half asleep while sitting in the chair. I put those aside and went on to the next one.

Oh, my, what else could I find? Next up was the Cooking with Horse and Buggy. This one had some recipes for cooking with cast-iron skillets. Oh, I found one for cooking over an open fire. Looking on through the book, I found a manual for a sweeper, a mixer, and a clock radio which probably are no longer in their possession and might have been sold at the auction. There were a few award certificates for accomplishments that it looked like the girls had won. On one award, there was a name Katherine, and the other name was Madalyn with a last name of Moore. They had won a spelling bee at school. Inside of it were several pictures of bees. *This was cute*, I thought. So they must have been good at spelling. Looking on, there was a handwritten paper which looked like a tractor and wagon agreement form. There were a few receipts attached to it.

So I flipped through the next cookbook *Camp Christian*, and it revealed some more recipes. At the bottom of every recipe there was a Bible verse. I found some business cards of local farm machinery places and a couple of poems about flowers. As I got to the end of the cookbook, there was a piece of folded newspaper clipping. I opened it up to find an obituary, yes, of Jedidiah Moore. It looked like it was just torn out instead of cutting it out of a newspaper. I added it to the envelope with the adoption papers.

I started searching the next cookbook *Sharing our Favorites*, which had several cookie and cake recipes in it, and some were spotted with dried-up oil and flour. It also had some recipes written on index cards. At the back of the book was a hanky that had crocheting around the edge. The hanky was stained a little, so I took it out of the book and out fell a ring. Oh my goodness! I observed the hankey and picked up the ring. It looked like a wedding band. Nothing fancy, just a gold wedding band. Huh! This was puzzling to say the least. I folded the ring back up into the hankey and put the ring and hankey in the envelope with the adoption papers. Do you suppose this was Mrs. Moore's wedding ring?

As I went on and took the next one, *Cooking with Foil*, I found several pieces of foil in narrow strips along with a cardboard book marker with a poem on it. *What could these strips of foil be used for*, I wondered. This had some recipes for cooking on an outdoor grill. All the ingredients were wrapped up in foil. This sure would be easy to clean up. I may check out those recipes.

I went on to the next cookbook, *Church of Christ*, which was the spiral plastic ring one. This one had tabs for each category such as bread, cookies, main dishes, drinks, and a glossary. It was smaller than the rest of them. I could see some papers sticking out of it, and they were recipes; so I stuck them back in the book. There were more newspaper clippings of recipes. Some of the pages were stuck together. There were a couple cancelled checks to some seed companies and a check to a gas company. The last on was to Carol

Lynn Watterson for one thousand dollars, however, it had VOID written across the entire check. Why would the Moore family be giving Carol Waterson a thousand dollars?

Boy, aren't these cookbooks getting interesting, I thought to myself.

The *Farmhouse Kitchen* and *Becky's Favorite Recipes* were the last two books to check. These looked like something from the Amish country. I checked the first one and found a child's drawing of a swing and a slide. It was drawn on art paper and scribbled on it was, "To Mommy." There were a couple recipes clipped from a newspaper. Next was the Becky's cookbook. It was the newest one of the bunches and was in good condition. It was shiny and washable. I looked through the pages and it too contained clippings of recipes. At the end of the book was an envelope that was sealed and taped. Well, since all of this is mine, I took a knife and opened it. There was what looked like a long grocery list and attached to it was cash, yes, cash. I took it out of the envelope and counted it. There were fives, tens, twenties, and even three fifty-dollar bills. I counted it twice and found that there was three hundred and fifty-two dollars.

I thought to myself, *This is real money not fake. What is it with this woman?* Even though they were sealed in that envelope, they should have been put somewhere more secure than a cookbook. What an unsolvable mystery this has become. Well, the cookbooks must have been her secret hiding place. No one else did the cooking but her, so who would find these things?

I showed the money to Patty and the first thing she asked was, "Is it real?"

"Well, I am sure they are," I said softly. I put all the cash together and decided to talk to Allen about it. The total cash was $1,052. Wow! Why? I thought. My gosh, why would she keep this money all this time, when she could have deposited it at a bank and drawn interest on it. I bet she saved all of these for her daughters but never got the right time to give it to them. I wondered when she was going to give these to them, her daughters, that is. Just think of the interest this would have accumulated over the years. I guess she never thought about the interest back then. Patty looked them over as did I. It looked like she used the cookbooks as her safety deposit box.

I told Patty, "I will put them in my safe along with the coins, and we will take them over to Allen and ask him about them. Maybe he still has an address for these ladies, and I can send this stuff to them. They probably never knew that their mother kept them."

Patty beamed. "Do you have to send the money back to them?"

I told her, "It is not ours unless the ladies cannot be found."

She reported, "Yes, it is. You bought the box of things."

I continued, "Well, I will check with Allen and Lynn and see what they have to say."

Patty quickly responded, "Let us take them over now."

I replied, "Not tonight, it is seven o'clock, and they are probably eating supper."

She quizzically mentioned, "Speaking of supper . . ." Just then, Brian pulled up. Patty yelled! "MY BROTHER'S HOME!"

He was walking up the driveway, and she went running to him and was excited to see him and gave him a big hug. I believe sometimes she gets excited to see her brother because she has a longing for a father's love, and he chose to not have any connections with his kids. He always looks out for her and is there to help her when she needs it. Patty was always giving Brian hugs, but he did not freely give them back. The only thing Brian didn't help her with was playing ball. He did take her to some of her games and stayed and watched her play.

As I took the last cookbook from the box, I found a small wooden box and a cardboard shirt box. The wooden box had a little clasp on it. I thought to myself, *Now what could this be?* I carefully opened it to find three razor-blade knives. It looked like a set of wood-carving knives. Each resembled a razor blade and were very sharp and had silver handles. *Huh! So unique*, I thought. I wonder if the father was a carver.

I opened the shirt box to find it full of aprons. Beautiful hand made aprons. I took them all out of the box, and there were three aprons all made from the same printed material. They all three had a top and then the bottom wrapped halfway around. The ties were long so it could be wrapped around and tied in front like a bow. There were deep pockets in the front of all of them and as I checked them out there was a hankey with a crochet ruffle around the edge. One was larger than the other two. *Wow!* I thought to myself. *She made them all look alike aprons for herself and her daughters. What a wonderful caring mother she was.* However, I am sure since they are all grown up, they wouldn't want them now. They wouldn't think of wearing them now and since they didn't like many of the things their mother made, they probably wouldn't like these. Oh well, I can save them to use when my grandchildren come to help grandma cook. I do hope it will be a while since Brian is only 20 and Patty is only 15. I am not ready to be a grandma yet. I did recognize pieces of the material on the comforter.

Since the sun was going down, and a cool evening was setting in, I put all the cookbooks back into the box. I put all the papers back in the envelopes. I went inside the house and found a large envelope and put all of the papers into it.

Patty started catching lightning bugs and putting them in a glass jar. Brian told her to let them loose because they will die in there. She and he watched as each crawled out of the glass and flew away to freedom. Boy, don't take much to amuse them, but it is assuring that they enjoy each other's company and it is comforting to see nature transpiring. I love the glow that the lightning bugs give off. It is so fascinating the way their body lights up. Another one of God's amazing creations.

We all went into the house, and I warmed up the spaghetti and garlic bread we had for dinner. We all ate a dish of ice cream for dessert. While eating, just the three of us, we told of thing that happened with each of us that day. I told them of the mysterious item I found in the cookbooks.

These cookbooks provided a peek into the past. It's fun and it's educational for kids as well as adults, to learn about simpler times, not necessarily easier times in some ways. I had showed Patty the old recipes and some she liked and some she did not think she would like.

I believe I will save all the papers with recipes on them and type them up and add them to one of those cookbooks with the plastic fastener.

Life is interesting. Just when you think you have mastered an aspect of life, it seems there are more challenges thrown your way. You make choices in your life in order to have the life you want. There are times that I live my life as an adventure. Like going to the auction, I chose it as an adventure, and I approached it as a choice to satisfy my longing for finding the treasures in the box lot items. It doesn't matter how old I get; I still wake up every morning grateful to be alive and healthy, and passionate about making the most of the day. It wasn't until I sat down to write this book that I thought about how I got that way.

Monday came sooner than I wanted it to, so it was back to work for me; and since school had just started, it was back to school for Patty. Brian was working full-time on the line crew at the local fertilizer facility since he graduated a couple years ago. He worked for the same company that I worked for, only I worked in the office, and he worked in the plant. I went down to see Lynn at work and asked her about the items I had found. She reminded me that anything and everything that I got at the auction was supposed to be mine.

I told Lynn, "I would like to find the owner of these papers, certificates, the adoption certificates, the money, and the coins to see if they would want them." I commented, "Don't you think they would want the historical papers about themselves?"

She responded, "Well, I am sure they would want the cash and the coins, but I do not know about the old papers. Since they did not know they were in there, why notify them?" That's true, I responded, "That is a good point. But I guess I would feel better if the family had these, since it is about their life growing up." She told me she would look to see if there was a name and address of the contact person on the signed document from their auction. She thought it was the husband of one of the daughters that lived there. They did not live around here, and she thought they lived in California somewhere. I guess, I will not feel right taking someone's possessions such as these. I would just throw them away Lynn responded.

She concluded, "Why don't you bring those things over tonight and let your brother look at them, and we will see what the coins are worth?"

I pondered this the whole day while working at my desk. I feel that I should try to contact someone in the family about all the papers. I believe I will not send the money or the papers until I can verify an address. If they respond to my letter, then I will send everything to them.

I stopped by and picked up Patty and changed from my work clothes. We got over to Allen and Lynn's around 6:00 p.m. I showed him the envelope that contained all the papers and the money. He carefully examined each piece and read what was legible. "These don't look that important so why would they need them?"

I replied, "the adoption papers and baptism papers are important."

"But they don't know anything about them," he laughed. "So why bother?" He laid the papers aside and took the baggies with the coins.

He laid all the coins out onto the counter and one by one he examined the coins and checked in his book. So here is what you've got with the coins, he said.

1 silver dollar dated 1921 Liberty Crown and eagle on the back.
2 silver dollars dated 1947 Eisenhower on front with Liberty on the back.
1 silver dollar dated 1947 Liberty only with eagle on back.
2 silver dollars dated 1922 Liberty with crown and eagle on the back.

Allen got out his magnifying glass and looked closer at the coins. He said that the coins looked good and the older one might be worth something. He laid those in a stack and set them aside.

Then he went to the Kennedy half dollars. "NOW LETS TAKE A LOOK!" he hollered in his deep stern auction voice. He laid them out on the counter one by one. He pondered and grunted, "Let's see what JFK is worth." He announced everything that he was seeing, he spoke as if he was auctioning them off or something.

"One Kennedy half dollar dated 1974 JFK on one side and USA and Eagle on back. It looks like it is in good shape," and he laid it aside.

"One Kennedy half dollar dated 1971 JFK on one side and an Eagle on the back. This one looks good," and he laid it aside.

One Kennedy half dollar dated 1968 JFK on front and an

American Eagle on the back. This one was shiny, the shiniest of them all." He laid it aside.

One Kennedy half dollar dated 1964 JFK on one side and American Eagle on the back. Okay!" He stacked all of them up in a pile and put them aside.

I mentioned to Allen that I washed the coins in baking soda and dish soap to get the black coal dust and dirt off them. He commented, "For really old coins, there is a certain kind of cleaner for those." He took out a soft piece of cloth and started polishing the buffalo nickels.

Next, he put all the buffalo nickels out on the bar. There were nine of them. There were four of them dated 1919 with an Indian on one side and a Buffalo on the other side. There were four of them dated 1938 with the Indian and Buffalo on the other side. Allen told us this was the last year of the buffalo nickel. After 1938, they quit making the buffalo nickel. The last buffalo nickel in my group had a date of 1923. It had an S engraved just below the year. Allen said this is interesting. It might be worth more since it has an S on it. He looked closely at it with his magnifying glass.

Allen looked over each of the coins again carefully and some he used his magnifying glass again and searched for letters or imperfections on the coins. He announced, most of the coins, if I were to guess, had a value of under one hundred dollars except the silver dollars. Their values varied because of the date.

Last was my bag of twenty pennies. He took each one out of the bag and turned them heads up so he could see the year. Most of them were in the 1990s but a couple were dated 1974 and 1969. There was one dated 1900.

I asked him, "So if you find their value, who do you sell them to? Will the bank buy them from you?"

He informed me, you let me worry about that and if they are a collector's, I know where to sell them online. So, you do want to sell them, he asked. Excitedly I answered yes.

Lynn had looked in her files when she got home and found a name and address of the guy she spoke with about holding the auction. They lived in San Francisco, California.

Lynn advised me, "I cannot give you the name and address because of confidentiality to the family. Why don't you let me write them a letter from the auction, and I will explain that you found some papers of value. They can contact me, if they want the items sent to them. That way, there is no name and address given out that should not be given."

I contemplated and decided. "That sounds like a good plan. I do not want you to get in trouble for giving out their address," I answered.

I took the papers but left the coins with Lynn. I told her how thankful I was that we had family that could help with stuff like this. I told Allen, "I wished you would have another auction like this one."

Patty and I said our goodbyes and headed home. But on the way home, we stopped by Mom's to check to see if she needed anything. She lived close and it was on our way home. I told Mom about the papers and cash and coins that I had found, and that Allen and Lynn were checking on them. I told her about the cookbooks, silverware, vases, and baskets.

Patty mumbled, "Are you going to tell her about the comforters?"

I suggested, "Well, you can tell her." And she loudly told her that she and Brian have new, well-used comforters and pillow shams for their beds. Oh, Mom was hard hearing even with her hearing aids, so everything you wanted to say to her you had to speak loudly. Mother teasingly told her, "Now you will have to keep your bed made." She laughed and so did Patty.

Mother said she would like to see all the cookbooks and to bring them over sometime and she would look through them.

I saw Lynn at work and told her that I appreciated her contacting the family in California, and we will just have to wait and see if they respond.

I told her, "I do not anticipate an answer from them, but it is reassuring that we tried to get in touch with them." She announced, "Let us wait around three or four weeks to see if they respond."

My brother called me and was able to verify the values of the silver dollars and that varied. "When you are ready to get rid of them, let me know," he proposed. I replied, "I am now. I do not like having this much money around the house. You keep the silver dollars and see if you can sell them."

Allen was interested in the old coins. He enjoys checking on their values. He was going to see if he could sell them online. Allen announced, "Buffalo nickels, some of them are valuable. Coin collectors are looking for them. One of those pennies is a two-cent piece. Now that is a collector's item."

I told Allen to keep all the coins and see if he could get anything out of them. That is unless we hear from the family, and they want that stuff back along with the money. No use building up hopes of them becoming mine until I can verify that they are mine. You know Allen acknowledged, that whatever you purchase at an auction belongs to the purchaser. Still, there is a lot of money involved here if the coins are valuable and I am sure they are. I will not be satisfied that it is mine until I hear from the family. Plus, there is a lot of history about themselves that perhaps might be valuable to them.

I had occasional daydreams of how I would spend the cash once

I verified, that it was mine. The total cash of the coins was eight dollars and sixty-five cents. However, I hoped that Allen would find someone that was a coin collector. Then there was the cash I found in the cookbooks. I kept thinking to myself; I have the house mortgage payment coming due, insurance on the car, and numerous repairs on the car. This extra cash would help me a lot. Usually, I got my brothers to do the routine oil changes and other minor repairs on my car. However, it needed new tires and I was told you should get an alignment if you are going to buy new tires. Plus, Patty probably needs some work done on her truck. Well, these repairs will just have to wait. Yes, wait for a miracle.

As the weeks went by, I put the letter to California in the back of my mind. After the third week, Lynn called me and explained that the envelope came back "Return to Sender." I yelled, "YOU DID! I MEAN IT DID!"

Lynn responded with, "That means they have relocated, and the content of that envelope is yours. Congratulations, sis. Allen wants to get you a better deal with those silver dollars so I will let him talk to you about them."

We went over to Allen and Lynn's that following weekend, and Allen stated he had some good news for me. "Those six silver dollars are worth around five to six hundred dollars total, and I know someone that will take them off your hands. So are you sure you are ready to get rid of them? The half dollars are worth twenty-five dollars each, and the buffalo nickels are all worth around forty to fifty dollars to one hundred dollars. There were some wheat pennies, and they are worth maybe ten to twenty dollars each. Now the two-cent penny, it is worth around one hundred dollars. It is really nice. So here you go," he continued, "and I will let you know when I sell them." He jiggled the bag of coins and smiled and laid them on my lap.

I thanked him for his work and gave him back the coins and asked him to sell them and get out of them whatever he could. "If there are some you want for your personal collection, just keep them. Why don't you keep the two-cent piece and add it to your collection?" He said okay and thanks.

Lynn asked, "What are you going to do with all those papers?"

I remarked, "I have no idea. Some of them look important and should mean something to the two girls. Wish I could find some way for them to get them."

Patty was playing with their German Shepherd's as I asked, "Are you about ready to go home? You have not had time to do your homework, so we had better get started on it." We added our goodbyes and gave hugs to both before we left. I thanked them again for all their information and hard work.

I hashed the situation of the legal document of the adoption and other papers. So how in the world would I be able to get the papers to them? I will sleep on it and see if I can think of something.

The next morning, I awoke with an idea for those papers from the cookbooks. I told Patty, "Well, what about taking a few of the important papers, the adoption papers and their baptismal papers, their baby pictures, and the wedding ring, and putting them into a glass jar. That is if they will fit. Take the jar and bury it at their parents', Jedidiah and Margarette Moore, grave. Sounds kind of fishy doesn't it."

Patty agreed, "That's fishy all right. Well, maybe, just maybe, their family would visit their parents' grave and put flowers on it sometime. They might fly home for a visit with family and maybe around Memorial Day or Mother's Day they might go to the cemetery."

Now, the big question, "How do I find their grave?" I went on the computer at work and got a listing of all the cemeteries around Richwood. Well, there were three main ones in the area. Clairbourne, Old Richwood, and Hamilton Cemetery. And there were four more smaller ones. I wonder if these are graveyards. If it is on a church yard, these are graveyards. If it is just a space with graves and no church, those are called cemeteries. So, in addition to those three, there were Maskill, Price, Somersville, and Temple Cemeteries. Well, well, well! This may be quite an undertaking. So I looked it up in Find a Grave, and found that Jedidiah Moore was buried at the Bethlehem Cemetery located in Richwood, Ohio. Okay, now I need to do some more research and find out where Bethlehem Cemetery is located. After doing some internet searching, I found that it is now called Clairbourne Cemetery. Okay, this is good news. After some more internet research, I found where this one was located. I was going through the papers that I wanted to put into the jar and came across Jedidiah Moore's obituary. Yes, there it said he was buried at the Bethlehem Cemetery. I thought about the adoption papers and the baptismal papers, their baby pictures and of course the hankey and the ring. I got one of those largemouth quart jars and a flat and a ring for the jar. I could get everything into the jar even though it was tight. Now, I need to write a note. Okay, what should I say? I kept practicing as what to say. I went through three papers and tore them up and started over. I finally came up with this sincere explanation.

To the family of Jedidiah and Margarette Moore, I give to you these papers. I thought they may be important to some of you. I bought a box of Margarette's cookbooks at their auction and found these items inside the cookbooks. Not knowing how to get in touch with the family, I wanted to find a way to get these to you the best way I know. I thought they would be of importance to the family. God bless you and your family. Starling Rose

I put the note inside the jar so the note could be read from outside the jar. I didn't put any of the money in the jar, just in case someone other than the family would open the jar and take out the cash and throw the jar away. If they wanted more information, they could look me up. Now to head to the cemetery. It was early Saturday morning, and there was a slight chill in the air. I told Patty where I was going and what I was doing, and she wished me good luck at finding the grave. I asked her if she wanted to go, but she said she doesn't like cemeteries or graveyards. They are creepy, she snickered. I got the spade shovel from the garage and took an extra fuchsia geranium flower and a couple marigolds with me along with a bucket, a half bag of potting soil, and my little flower shovel and drove over to Clairbourne.

The town was what I call a fly by night town. You have to keep your eyes open wide or you will miss the town which actually was quite small, so the graveyard was not hard to find. There were several sites to look for as I read the names on the tombstones. After twenty minutes of searching, I thought I had checked every stone there, to no avail. Off in a distance, there is this grave that was under a big tree that hung over the grass, shading the stone. There it was, a dark-black colored stone with specks of glitter that twinkled as bits of sunlight shown through the big tree. It had Jedediah and Margarette Moore on it and in the middle was their wedding date of August 19, 1923. There was a flower on the grave, but it was dried up from lack of water and care. I pulled it up and put the geranium in its spot and put the marigolds on each side of it and watered it well and added lots of potting soil. I pulled some weeds and grass away from the stone. There was some dried-up mulch in the front and nothing in the back. So I dug a hole, deep enough to almost hide the jar and the only thing showing was the rim of the jar. *There, that looks nice with the new soil around it and so does the grave*, I thought. I gathered up my stuff and put everything in the bucket and said a little prayer that the right person would find the jar. On my way to the car, I read some of the names on the tombstones. Some were unique and some were common names. So there, I felt that I had done what I could and felt better about myself that perhaps the jar would be found by the right person. If it is meant to be, it will happen.

CHAPTER 4

Life's Challenges

A life is simply a series of little lives, each of them lived one day at a time and every single one of these days has choices and consequences. Piece by piece those decisions help transform the people we become. Challenges show themselves in many ways.

As I write this book, I find myself looking deeply into the reservoir of my memory and seeing reflections of the things I haven't thought about in many years. Should any of my story touch anyone, anywhere, in any way, I shall consider myself abundantly blessed.

I grew up in a poor family and was raised by uneducated parents. I was forced to adapt to life in a household where you were never really sure who was in charge. I always pictured myself as the one person and the only person besides God who I could count on to design the life I wanted to live and make it a reality. Everything that has happened to me is the result of conscious choices that I made. Some of which, I must tell you were difficult to make and scary to live with and not always the right choices.

I wake up every morning and I thank God for everything that is good, right and true in my life. I am thankful for the two fine children who remind me every day of the rightness of my mission here on earth.

Coming from a family of ten children with minimal income from my father, and hand-me-down clothes, I was determined to make something of myself and my children. Here you are "Starling Rose!" It is my time to make a statement.

Some of my life was growing up in the fifties and sixties and a home with lots and lots of kids at which I helped raise, babysit them, and shared anything and everything that I had with my sisters and brothers. I was number three in a large and boisterous family of five girls and five boys. There was seldom any alone time.

When I was just fifteen, I went and stayed in a foster home with an elderly lady that was deaf. Someone from the Health Department put the three oldest children in my family into foster homes because my father did not make enough money to support ten kids at the time.

The lady that I went to live with was so nice; she was somewhere in her mid to late '70s. I was her ears. She was deaf and a widow. We communicated by writing things on a tablet until eventually I learned to sign. I called her Aunt Nellie even though she was not related to us. She could also read your lips quite well. Her family lived in the Columbus area, and Aunt Nellie wanted to stay in her homeplace after her husband passed away. Nursing homes were not very plentiful then and that was Aunt Nellie's last resort. While there, I also cleaned house and graded papers for a neighbor lady that was a schoolteacher, for fifty cents an hour. I kept my room clean and made my bed every day.

I would go home on some weekends. Being away from my mother, father, and brothers and sisters was the hardest thing. I would often daydream and wonder what they were doing. Are they missing me like I miss them? I missed being part of their lives as they grew up. But I lived in a beautiful home with running water and an indoor bathroom and my own room. I never had much growing up, including guidance from a mother and father. Because there were so many of us, there was less parental attention. So this taught us to be more self-reliant. At fifteen, I became my own person, including parent or guardian, and I made my own decisions about the things in my life. No one to argue with or complain to. Therefore, I grew up fast. My older sister, Leigh lived one house down from me, also in a foster home. We visited back and forth and shared specific events in our lives. She was three years older than me and had her driver's license and a car. I went to church on most Sunday's because I usually went with sister Leigh and her foster parents.

When I was eighteen, I fell in love with the first guy that paid any attention to me. We dated for ten months, then I married him at the age of eighteen. He grew to be an abusive alcoholic husband, and we had to live with his father and adult brother and sister. He never had the ambition to get a home to raise our family.

We had two beautiful children, a boy Brian, and a girl Patty. The ideal family. Right! We were married seven exceedingly difficult years. Then he got tired of me, I guess. You know, the wandering eye. Plus, being an alcoholic, you know how that can lead to hardships and tribulation. I was always busy working and taking care of our children. He had an affair with a woman from where he worked. Shortly after our divorce, they got married.

Brian was just seven years old when his father and I got divorced, and Patty was just a toddler and almost two years old. We moved in with my father and mother for a while. Mother just loved spoiling the kids.

Eventually, I saved enough to get us an apartment in Marysville so I would be closer to work and the kids' school. I was able to find a kind and caring babysitter. She was an older lady and lived by the old-fashion rules. This taught them how to respect their elders and do what your parent says.

I was worried about how the split up would affect the kids. Let's face it, telling them about starting over and starting out a new life together, just the three of us, isn't always a walk in the park. As time passed by, their father did not want anything to do with them while they were young, so I played both father and mother the best way I could. Even though they both had their own room, they knew that if they were bothered about something, they could always climb in bed with Mom, and we would cuddle. Cuddling and talking about our feelings got us through.

I eventually bought a used trailer in the local trailer park in Marysville. This gave us a little distance from the neighbors so close to us. After a few months in the trailer, my younger sister, Karen, moved in with us and babysit the kids and went to school. This helped me financially and helped her emotionally and gave her a home away from home. She grew to be my sister and my daughter; however, I was only ten years older than her.

All children need a laptop—not a computer but a human laptop. Moms, grannies, grandpas, aunts, uncles, friends, and neighbors. Someone to hold them, read to them, teach them, and best of all to sit on their lap. Loved ones who will embrace them and pass on their life experiences and knowledge of previous generations. Being a single mom and raising two kids by myself was quite challenging. I had some great help from their aunts, uncles, and grandmother when times would get tough.

I worked full-time at an office job at a local fertilizer place. I volunteered for all overtime when it was available. Living in

Marysville, we lost connection with God and the church we grew up in.

I missed the church family and my connections with the Lord. Occasionally, we would go with Mom to her church on special events and holidays. She attended the church in West Mansfield close to where she lived. Deep in my heart I always knew the Lord was looking out for me. I love to sing gospel songs and get that warm feeling in my heart. I do not know where I heard this, but I thought that divorced girls don't go to church or are not welcome. Like I was branded or something. I did not cheat on my marriage vows; he did. So, I just accepted it.

Mother did not drive, so she walked to the Baptist church when the weather was good. When I went with her, I would drive her down, unless it was a beautiful morning and we walked down. She eventually got a job cleaning the church to make extra money. She was a great house cleaner and did a great job at cleaning the church, and it was close to where she lived in West Mansfield.

Life endlessly offers us a chance to set new directions, new goals, and in the process, we grow and change. We can do anything we want to if we stick to it long enough. We do not always see it at the time, but the struggles of life are one of our greatest blessings. It makes us patient and sensitive, plus teaches us that although the world is full of many challenges, we can still overcome them.

As time went on, we all grew stronger and learned to live with life's changes. I got a few promotions at work and had a little more income. We grew in knowledge and learned to trust people in different ways. I was able to take some night classes to better myself at various jobs at work. I came close to obtaining my two-year associate degree.

However, we kept getting by even though there were times I lived from paycheck to paycheck. There were a lot of times that I would talk to God about what bills I should pay next. That was why I took the job at the restaurant.

Brian never asked for much. What repairs he needed for his truck, he would pay for them himself most of the time. His uncles were there for him when he needed repairs as they offered him the guidance. Patty, on the other hand, was always needing something. She liked to participate in sports and wanted to be active with her classmates. She was a good student and got along with most kids; however, she never let anyone walk all over her.

I was single for five years after that.

My second marriage was quite repulsive in many ways. My children were young and needed a father figure, and I needed someone to care for me and help me with my kids and share the beautiful things in life. We had enough love to offer someone if they would just care for us and share our life together.

I met this guy at work. He worked on my computer and programs in my job. We dated awhile and did things with the kids and went to auctions together and we married eight months after we met. Just before we were married, Lewis had taken a job in his hometown and was relocating. After the small wedding, we loaded up everything and moved to a town in southern Ohio. The kids liked him, and I thought he liked me and the kids. He had no children and was not around many children. He did not understand how children have a need to be loved and cared for. Lewis only understood discipline and that he did every time he could. Do not get me wrong, children need discipline, but they need a loving kind that will teach them right from wrong. I appreciated his teaching them some discipline and respect as they were growing up. As time went on, I could see us drifting apart because I think he was jealous of the affection I showed my kids versus the affection I showed him. There are lots of different kinds and ways to show affection.

He lost his job with the company closing. I had an office job in a town close by, but it would not support us. He stated that he could draw unemployment for a while, until he found another job but was not sure he could support our family on unemployment. He knew that I could send them back to their father if I could not provide for them. As time went on, one difficulty led to another, so I decided to take my kids and go back home. This marriage only lasted five years.

So we moved back to the Marysville area in November of 1985. Brian had just turned sixteen the past September and Patty had just turned eleven the past August. My brother David was selling real estate as a side job, so I contacted him to look for me a house. And shortly after, we moved to a small town at the edge of Marysville. It was a on a main road, with a convenient store and pizza parlor rolled into one and a bar and restaurant downtown. There was a big building that used to be an auction barn. And at the edge of town was an old schoolhouse and ballfield. It was an older home and had three small bedrooms. *Good, just what we needed*, I thought. So we decided to call Broadway our home.

The house was a dark yellow with brown shutters around all the windows. It had the old shag carpet and dark paneling in all the rooms. There was linoleum in the kitchen and bathroom. Only two bedrooms had a closet, and they were both small. I had brother David make me a bigger closet. The house had an unattached garage/barn. It was so dilapidated that I would be afraid to put a car in it. There was .058 acres with the property. There was a nice shade tree in the back yard and a small deck on the back. It had a nice big porch across the front, and it was shaded by the trees off to the right. The basement was under the entire house but was deteriorating from the moisture collected in it. This is all we needed, so we tried to get everything moved into the house. Lewis, hubby number two, made a large down payment on the house so that my payments would be small.

I vowed to myself that I would give the kids as much love that I could since I had to play the part of father and mother again. I never wanted to put my trust in a man again. Men was something I could do without for a long time.

As I said, it is all about choices, and I made the choice to be sure that I had a strong and clear voice that was heard, and that I was treated with dignity and respect by my children and anyone that came into our life.

We took in some furniture from mother, aunts, and uncles and this was enough to get started. We brought our personal belongings from the home in the south. We even brought the dog, Apache, along with his doghouse. He was a loving border collie with the brightest and kindest brown eyes. He was mostly black, with some white and brown. He helped us all adapt to the new home and so did he.

Lewis brought some of the stuff up in his truck and helped us get moved in. He bought me a stackable washing machine with a dryer on top. I went to the auction in Plain City and found some more furniture.

I was able to get a job at the local fertilizer place again. That is the same place I worked before I left to move south. I had a good reputation as a hard worker. I had a very understanding boss in the distribution department that had a heart of gold. She helped me in many ways while allowing me to work overtime to keep my bills paid.

We had the usual challenges that a lot of families have in life. I learned how to balance my budget and my life and make a livable home for us. You know, the maintenance on your home, taxes and your car can get expensive and challenging for your budget. Luckily,

I had brothers that helped me with my car repairs when it needed fixed. I had this neighbor across the road that helped me with my furnace and plumbing needs. He would only charge me for parts and not the labor. I learned from Mother to keep a tidy house. I took Mother's trademark that she was adamant about and placed throw rugs around the house.

As the kids got older, I tried to get them to keep their rooms cleaned up but that was like talking to a brick wall. The older they got, the more chores I gave them around the house. Another neighbor across the road took Brian under his wing and offered to help him when he had work to do on his truck. He was a mechanic and taught Brian lots about his truck and engines. He also learned a lot from his uncles that loved to tinker with vehicles.

As much as I don't want to admit it (we never do.) there are a few things I wish I'd done differently. I felt like I was doing my best at the time. Being a mother is more than a phase in my life; for me it is a never-ending mission. I always wanted my children to have peace, joy and excitement along with pride about who they are or have become. There are so many responsibilities to parenting, and I always wanted to be sure I'd done everything I could not only to give them the basics of life they needed, to live with passion and gusto and kindness.

One time, while we were all away, the garage caught on fire. We were burning some trash out behind the garage in a big rusty metal barrel. There must have been some sparks that had fallen to the ground and the grass was so dry that it started burning all the grass up the fence row, which led up to the garage and then the garage. I don't know if it was me or Brian that was burning the trash. Anyway, we should have checked on it before going away and leaving it. The garage almost totally burned down and singed the siding on the back of the house. We were fortunate that the insurance paid everything. We got most the items that were burned, replaced with new. We had a used lawn mower, and the kids had some used bikes. Brian had a few truck parts and a couple tires in the garage. Boy those smelled nasty as they burned. They were able to get the garage fire out and sprayed down the back of the house. We got a new garage built, and they even poured us a small patio between the garage and the house. They were able to match up the yellow siding and replace the entire back of the house. We all learned our lesson from that.

I took on a waitress job so I could get some money ahead to pay our bills. I worked a few evening shifts after getting off at my regular job and some weekends. Evenings paid more in tips. The extra money helped with the upkeep on the house too. We had a gas furnace that took propane, so I had to get it filled periodically with what money I could spare. While working at this restaurant when my shift was over, and when we were cleaning up, I would bring home some apple cobbler for Brian and myself and some cherry cobbler for Patty. I would warm them up and, oh, they smelled good. This was quite a treat for them.

I struggled at times to make ends meet and prayed that I could get through these hard times. Patty wanted to play in the band, but I did not have the money for her to take lessons.

Then she wanted to play on the girl's high school softball team. I was able to get her signed up at a reduced rate. She wanted to play summer softball, and I could not afford that either. One of the coaches talked to me about her playing summer ball and they needed her because she was a good player on the high school team. He explained they would waive the charges for me if I would let her play. So I agreed to let her play, and I scraped up enough money to buy her a new ball glove.

It was time for Patty to get her license, and so she did and passed with flying colors. Now to find her something to drive before she wreaks havoc on my car. After careful searching and talking to my brothers, friends, and neighbors, I found her a small truck. Patty, being a tomboy, announced she would rather have a truck anyway. So I was able to find her a Ford Ranger that was black with white pinstripes down the side. It must have had a dandy radio in it because you could hear it in the house when she pulled in the driveway.

Brian went through some hard times with his big truck. It was a regular truck with big tires and jacked up suspension. He and I bought it from Uncle David. I helped him out the best I could with getting parts for it to keep it running and so did his uncles.

Brian had some difficulties in school sometimes, and I found out he was not doing his homework. So I had to have a talk with him, plus I had Uncle Allen talk to him too. He would listen to what Allen would say more than he would me. When I was not working, I would try to make time to work with him on his homework and so did Patty. He was making passing grades which satisfied Brian, but I know he could have done better if he tried and applied himself. I just wanted to get him through school and graduate.

Brian was able to work part-time at the local fertilizer place where I worked. He got on the lawn crew through the school program and made enough money to keep his truck running and bought himself the essentials.

Being through two unsuccessful marriages, I was determined to get my two beautiful children, raise them to adulthood somehow and on my own with the help of the Lord. As a single mom, I have found God to be full of grace and sufficient for what I need. That doesn't come easily, however. It takes a conscious effort to reach out for Him and to believe He can answer those needs in my daily reality. I eventually overcame the saying that divorced women are not welcome in church. Patty and I started attending the country church that I was baptized at when I was just thirteen. Everyone accepted us just as if we were family, so we continued to attend.

We all have a past; we all have had to make choices that maybe were not the best ones. None of us are completely innocent, but we get a fresh new start each day to be a better person than we were yesterday.

I am stronger because I had to be the parents. I am smarter because of my mistakes. I am happier because of the sadness I have known, and now wiser because I have learned. Life is all about facing new challenges. Challenges are what make life interesting. Overcoming them is what makes them meaningful.

There still have been many tears, many days of excruciating loneliness and the profound need to share the load of life. God is always there through those times.

Chapter 5

The Comforter

The responsibilities of life, whether it be my own or someone else's, we need to understand that we oversee our own destiny through the choices we make in this life journey.

As the years passed, we continued to make a home for ourselves and settled into the small local town. Brian was working at a local lawn care company full time. Patty was working there also through the school-work program at mowing lawns. She was going to graduate from high school this year. My gosh, where did the time go. It was always important for my kids to know that I will be there for them forever. We can either reject our kids coming of age and pretend they're still little kids who cannot live without us, or we can accept that they are growing up into adults we hoped they'd become and get on with their lives.

One morning, Patty woke up with a sick stomach and a fever. I believe she was coming down with the flu or something. I gave her some Pepto-Bismol, and she swallowed it down in a gulp because it tasted nasty. I took a vacation day from work to stay home with her and as the day went on, she was able to eat some chicken noodle soup and drink some Seven-Up. Well, she had just gotten her soup down but began to feel nauseated.

She yelled, "Mom, my stomach feels funny!"

I hollered, "Run to the bathroom before you throw up." And then she threw up in her bed—all over herself and all over her blankets and, yes, her comforter. I stripped her bed and put them in a basket to be washed while she took a shower to get the smell off herself. Oh, did it ever smell! It almost made me sick just smelling it.

I told her, "You can sleep on the couch until I get your sheets and blankets washed. Take a pan with you in case you feel like vomiting again."

It was mid-October, and the weather was still warm throughout the day. So I thought I could hang the sheets out on the clothesline. Now the big bulky comforter, I had washed it a few times before and was able to get it into the washer if I washed it by itself, but I had never dried it in the dryer. I noticed that it was fading and getting kind of thin in places from washings. Oh well, maybe it will last one more winter. I decided to wait until tomorrow to wash the comforter, since it was a Saturday.

I continued to take care of Patty and made up her bed when her sheets were dry. They sure smelled fresh from the sunshine beaming down on them although some clouds were setting in. Patty was feeling much better and refused to stay on the couch. She watched a little bit of TV then was up roaming around outside and playing with Apache. *Good, he needed to get some exercise,* I thought. Brian had gone over to Uncle Allen's to work on his truck. Allen was like a big brother to Brian. After all, they were only five years apart.

Saturday morning, I had washed the comforter, I wondered if

it would dry enough on the clothesline today. The batting inside of it was losing its puffiness from numerous washings. The washing machine was making this banging noise and it was not level, so I opened the lid and straightened it out some and it continued to wash. I noticed that some of the batting was coming out from a whole that was along the side of the comforter.

Well, there were clouds moving in and turning the color of charcoal. Thunder and flickers of lightning were bouncing across the sky in the backyard. It was starting to rain. With this storm setting in, I could not hang the comforter outside, so I thought I would give it a try in the dryer. The comforter was bulky and because it was wet it was extremely heavy. As I was pulling it out of the washer, I found a couple twenties and a fifty-dollar bill fall onto the floor in front of the washer. OMG, this must have fallen out of someone's pants pocket from a previous wash. I did not think either of the kids would have that much cash in their pants pocket, but I would check with them since Brian just got paid. He did not have a checking account, so he always paid cash for everything. I managed to get the comforter into the dryer, and it had room to tumble. Since I only had the small stackable washer and dryer, they did not hold many clothes. So I was washing about every other day or two.

Life takes on radical twists and turns and hopes and dreams shift as people enter different phases of their lives. The sun was going down, illuminating a kaleidoscope sky as I noticed the rain had stopped and I admired the beautiful rainbow that stretched across the sky over the back yard. It was still to damp to hang the comforter outside. Patty was hanging out over at the ballpark with her friends.

The comforter had been in the dryer about thirty minutes, so I opened the door to the dryer to check if it was getting dry. What?

Wow! "Oh. My. Gosh!" I shouted. What in the world was happening? I declared.

As I opened the door, a mountain of money came falling out the door. Lots and lots of bills. I looked around me to see if this was a joke! No one was here but me. There were several fives, tens, twenties, and fifties; and I even saw a hundred-dollar bill! *What is going on here,* I mumbled to myself.

As I pulled out the comforter, more money came with it and more money was stuck inside it and it clung to the comforter and the dryer. The cash was nice and clean, I thought to myself, as I looked at some of the dates on the bills, they were dated in the late '60s to '70s. I wrestled with the thought, "Is it counterfeit?" I don't know how to tell. I kept pulling and picking up more money, and more money. Finally, I got a clothes basket and put the comforter into the basket with money stuck and sewed inside of it. I continued to pull money out of the dryer and even the dryer lint screen had money stuck to it. *This was not happening to me,* I thought. *Someone pinch me because I must be dreaming.*

I grabbed the laundry basket and dumped the heavy comforter into it and a smaller basket to put the money into. I finally got the dryer cleaned out, as far as I could see. I then started examining the comforter and noticed several holes and tears in it, and money and wet batting coming out of it. Some of the money was still sewed inside of it. I took my scissors and started clipping the stitches that held it together. As I looked, there was small stacks of cash that were sewn into the batting that was in the comforter. So I started tearing open the holes and pulling out more cash. Lots of tens and twenties stacked together. Another hole I found fifty's and one-hundred-dollar bills. *What can this be?* I asked myself.

Well, well, well. I recalled, I wish those ladies at the auction could see what their ugly comforter was producing. Several questions kept running through my mind. Is this mine to keep or do I have to turn it in to the ladies at the auction. Oh, I remember now. They moved and we do not know how to get in touch with them. The letter that Lynn sent them a few years ago, came back stamped "Return to Sender." Humm, I remember that I buried that jar at the gravesite. I should go over sometime soon and see if it ever got dug up. I wondered if the family ever visited the grave. Oh well, I should be concentrating on the mess I have in front of me. After several clippings and tearing of the comforter, I thought I was done.

By the time I was finished, the comforter was in shambles, the picnic basket was full of money, and the clothes basket was full of bits and pieces of the comforter along with the batting and stuffing. I decided I should sort through the basket and organize the cash so I could count how much was there, for curiosity's sake. Boy ole boy. I've never seen this much money in my life. What am I going to do with it?

That is what the mother of the ladies at the auction meant when their mother wanted the girls each to have one of the comforters, the special comforters. As she was putting the comforter together, she sewed cash in between the strips of batting. Amazing! That is what made the comforter so heavy. What a thoughtful lady, I guess. To save all of this for their ungrateful daughters. Yet I questioned her sanity and her eagerness to complete two comforters this way. *I wonder why she would not put this into a bank or savings box?* I questioned. I sat there and looked at the stack of money in amazement. My hands started shaking because I felt that I should not be the one to have found it. I took and put all the denominations of cash together and began to count it. Each stack was super clean since it went through the washer. I've never seen so many bills. I need to calm down so I can count it.

I came to a total and I didn't think it was right, so I counted it again and wrote down the number of fives, tens, twenties, fifties, and one hundreds. The total of $8,300 kept coming up. Well, that cannot be right. So I counted it again and got the same number. Wow! Eight-thousand three hundred dollars. Kind of an odd number. My ole my! What should I do with it, and whom should I tell? I kept the money in the picnic basket. I felt so nervous, seeing that much money and I felt delirious. I gathered up the scraps of the comforter and put it in a garbage bag. Now what do I do? Do I call and report it to the police? I will call brother David; he will know what to do. David was brother number one of the five. I did not get an answer from him, but I left a message.

I decided to call my sister-in-law Lynn and asked her some questions because she knew a lot about rules for auctions. She worked at the same place I did. My questions were running wild. Should I give this to the ladies at the auction? Well, that was almost three or four years ago. Well, I cannot do that because they no longer live at the address Lynn had on file. Should I call the police and tell them? Do I give it back to Allen and Lynn? Lynn's line was busy, so I left a message.

Lynn finally called me and asked, "What's up and how is Patty doing?"

"Oh, she has recuperated because she is over at the ballpark playing ball."

"I have a few questions for you," I said.

"Okay. I hope I can answer," she replied.

"My first question is, when you buy an item at the auction and you find something in addition to what you bought it belongs to the purchaser, right?"

She replied, "Yes, if you buy something, like maybe a box lot, you have bought everything in that box."

"What if you buy something that was not in a box but was inside the item you bought?"

She answered, "It would all be yours. What is going on? You have got me curious now."

I asked her, "Do you remember that auction I went to over by Richwood? It was maybe three or four years ago."

Lynn replied, "Yes, you bought some baskets, I believe. Did you find something in one of those baskets? Ole, I remember, that was when you found those coins and cash in the cookbooks. Yell, Yell, I remember that one. That has been awhile."

I answered, "Well, it was not in the baskets, but it was in the comforter that I bought."

"Yes, yes," she stated. "I believe there were two of them, right? You still have them?"

"Well, I washed and dried Patty's comforter because she vomited on it. And when I opened the dryer, it fell apart."

"Oh no," she giggled. "The comforter fell apart."

"Wait a minute!" I shouted. "You will not believe this, Lynn. I opened the dryer and there were lots and lots of money spilling out of the dryer and hanging out of the comforter."

"WHAT!" she replied. "Money? Cash? OH MY GOSH! How much?" she asked.

"Well, I think I have it all out of the dryer," I told her. "As far as I can tell there was $8,300 sewed into Patty's comforter."

She chuckled, "SO EXCITING! You have got to be kidding me! That is an odd number," she replied.

"I know! What should I do with all this money?" I stammered.

Lynn replied, "Yes, yes, it is all yours. You bought the comforter as is."

"Mine? All mine?" I gasped.

She laughingly explained; Yes, yours and boy you were lucky. Why don't you go shopping at auctions for me sometime?

Then she asked me something that I did not think about.

How about the other one? You bought two of them. She quizzically commented.

Oh! Oh! I laughed. I forgot that I bought two of them. Yes, Yes, I beamed; It is on Brian's bed. I will have to check it out and I will let you know.

She laughingly exclaimed, "Wait till I tell your brother. He will be so surprised."

I replied, "Allen told me the comforters were ugly and that is why no one would bid on them."

"You know," Lynn replied, "that total seems odd . . . You sure you got it all out?"

I responded, "I thought I had it all out, but I should probably pull the washer out and check under it."

She repeated, "Well, it is all yours and we cannot get in touch with the family. You do with it as you please. However, as your brother would say, he could take it off your hands it you do not want it."

She laughed. I told her that I do not feel right taking all this money. That lady, she made those comforters for her daughters to surprise them. Yep, they were the "surprise comforters" all right.

"You bought the comforters and everything that goes with it," Lynn reminded me. "Now, go see if there is more cash in your dryer, oh, and see if Brian's has any."

I started to cry with joy and got this lump in my throat as I told Lynn, "Thank you so much."

She stammered, "You were the lucky one since you are the one that bought them. Do not worry about it and go and check the other one, I am curious!" she shouted. I thanked her for the information and told her I would call her back.

First, I pulled out the washer/dryer combo unit and sure enough there were some cash under it, and I got me a screwdriver and took the dryer vent off the back of the dryer and sure enough, there were a few twenties and some fifties and even some hundreds inside the vent. I replaced the dryer vent after cleaning the lint out and pushed the washer back into its place.

I wondered, "Now how on earth did the cash get out of the dryer?"

I sat at the table and counted the cash again, adding what I had found. Oh, boy, oh, boy. It totaled $9,910! Oh! MY GOSH!

So I started shaking inside again as I began to cautiously cut open the comforter on Brian's bed. Oh gosh! I pulled back the batting and there they were. Lots and lots of money. Several tens and twenties and one-hundred-dollar bills along with some fifties, and they were all stuck together. As I moved around the comforter, I found some fives, tens, twenties, and more fifties and hundreds.

As I was pulling out the cash, Lynn called me. I yelled, "Yes! YES! It has money in it too. I do not have it all out yet so I will let you know once I count it."

She laughingly replied, "GREAT! Keep counting!" Then she hung up.

As I was pulling out the money, I pulled out several one-hundred-dollar bills. Wow! I never seen this much money before. I filled the basket up again and then I sorted the bills so I could count them. Boy the comforter was looking bad. I took what was left of the comforter and put it into the garbage bag with the other one. Now to count out this one. I found another one-hundred-dollar bill in the last piece of stuffing I pulled out. After I got all the denominations sorted in each stack, I came up with a stack of fives, tens, twenties, fifties, and several hundreds. Wow, a total of $10,000. OMG! I thought this was a dream.

I called Lynn and told her that I found more cash under the washer and in the dryer vent and how much was in Brian's comforter. She was so amazed and happy for me that I found this. Patty's had $9,910.

"Wow! Ten thousand dollars! I cannot believe it!" she replied. "Just wait until I tell your brother."

"Oh! Oh! I remembered. There was a fifty and two twenties that fell out of the washing machine as I was putting it into the dryer. Well, that adds up to $10,000."

I walked around the kitchen awhile in amazement plus I was shaking inside. I put the cash back into the basket and took it in my bedroom. It wouldn't all fit in my little safe. What will I do with it? Then I started thinking of all the bills I could pay with it, and I could pay back those that had loaned me money. I had to calm down and face reality.

As I was gathering up the torn quilt that was in shambles, I thought about taking off the pillow shams because they will not match anything. Then again, I thought maybe I should keep them as a souvenir, or a memory of this occasion. Well, I laid them aside and I would see if the kids wanted them on their bed, so I put the pillows back into the shams.

CHAPTER 6

What to Do

So, I decided to sleep on it and pray about it and thank the Lord for this life experience. I would approach the situation in the morning on what to do with all that cash. The kids would be home because it was a Sunday. I fixed us some breakfast and told the kids I needed to have a family meeting.

Patty commented, "Oh my! What has Brian done now? Brian is in trouble," she sang. "Brian is in trouble."

Brian giggled to Patty. "ME! What makes you think it is ME? More like what has Patty done. You are the one that is in trouble!"

I calmed them down and assured them that it was neither of them has done anything. "I am the one that did something." I was so anxious to tell them yet wanted to keep them in suspense.

"So," I started to explain. "Well, I was washing Patty's comforter since she vomited on it." I added, "Boy, Patty, it smelled so nasty!"

Brian replied, "Well, I wondered where mine went too."

So I showed him the garbage sack full of washed-up strips of material and batting from the comforters. The bag smelled musty because the one comforter was still damp, although it was torn in pieces.

"So, it did not make it through the dryer," Patty stuttered.

Brian sneered, "Mine is missing too! That was so heavy and warm."

Then I showed them the picnic basket that had a small lid on each side.

I hesitated, "How do you like Abe Lincoln ($5's), how do you like Alexander Hamilton ($10), and how about something with Andrew Jackson on it ($20) or even Ulysses S. Grant ($50)?"

Patty mumbled, "What do you mean, Mom?"

I ignored her and went on. "So," I laughingly continued. "So I believe there is some pictures of Ben Franklin ($100) in here too."

Patty concluded, "Well, George Washington is on the one-dollar bill. Do you have a basket full of one-dollar bills?"

Then Brian chimed in and answered, "Yes, these are all presidents. What's up, Mom! There are some presidents on money and Abe Lincoln is on the ten-dollar bill," Brian replied. "I do not know the rest since I don't see many of the other money with presidents on them."

Brian said, "Do not tell me that basket is full of one-dollar bills?" Come on Mom.

"Well, well, you guys are getting warm," I smirked with a smile. "Look inside this, Brian!" I told him. I handed the basket to him.

He opened it, got this gleam in his eyes, and snickered, "Mom, where did you get all that money?"

Patty grabbed the basket from Brian and had a frown on her face as she peeked inside the other lid. She started giggling and giggling profusely.

"Wow! MOM! Wow! Where did you get this? I have never seen

this much money in all my life!" she shouted rather excitedly. "Tell us, Mom!"

"Mom, what did you do? Win the lottery or something?" Brian replied.

I had rubber-banded the cash in denominations. They both had a twinkle in their eyes as they awaited my reply. Brian smiled and laughed and shouted, "This seems like the stash from a bank robbery on *Bonanza* or *Gunsmoke*."

"Well," I began, "I was washing Patty's comforter and as I was putting it into the dryer, I found some money on top of it. Well, I did not think anything about it because I sometimes leave money in my pants pocket, and it comes out in the washing machine. I just figured it was left in the washing machine, so I stuffed your comforter into the dryer. As I was taking your comforter out of the dryer, out came all this cash along with the stuffing or batting and the comforter. I had to cut some of the threads that were through the money. Lots and lots of cash!" By this time, they are both grinning from ear to ear.

"Oh MY GOSH!" Patty exclaimed as she started dancing around in circles.

"All of this was in the blankets?" Brian shouted. "Why would someone put this inside a blanket?" he uttered. "I just don't understand it." I reminded them of a book I read about the Wild West. Sometimes the ladies would sew money into the hem of their petticoat because there were dangerous times when they were robbed.

They each took the stacks of money out of the basket and placed it on top of the table, thus, creating a tower of cash.

Brian asked, "Mom, how much is here?"

I told him $20,000 altogether but some were in the washing machine and some inside the comforter.

Patty remarked, "Oh my gosh, Mom. Was this in mine?"

I said, "Yes, there was $10,000 in yours, and $10,000 in Brian's."

"What are you going to do with it?" Brian asked.

"Is it yours to keep, Mom?" Patty asked.

I told them that I had talked to Aunt Lynn about it, and she acknowledged it is mine to keep. I bought the comforters as is, so it is mine. Besides, those ladies that was at the auction don't seem to be reachable.

"So," I told them, "I want to share it with you, guys."

They both started giggling and mumbling to themselves. Brian replied, "I like that idea, really good idea, Mom."

"But first, I want to save some to give in the collection plate at church. You know God should always come first in our lives. I have some bills that I want to pay off especially my credit card that I used to buy you Christmas last year. My car needs some work done on it and new brakes and tires and Brian, I believe you need new tires for your truck. Patty is going to need some work done on her truck. So, I need to find her some new tires also."

Boy did her eyes light up! "Hold on now, we will see what all needs done on it. Brian, how much do you think new tires would cost for your truck?" I asked.

"Well, they are called Ground Hog tires for a 1978, F150, so I will have to check with Uncle David and see if he might know where I can get some retread ones," Brian replied. "Since I got the truck from Uncle David, he would know. I am sure they are expensive. I will check and let you know. He needed the big tires for his jacked-up truck."

"Continuing," I responded, "I want to open a savings account at the Credit Union for each of you, and I will put $2,000 in each of your accounts," I announced. "But for today, I want the three of us to get dressed up and go out to a nice restaurant this evening. It has been a long time since we have been out to eat other than fast food. Now, I want both of you to promise me that you will not tell anyone that I have this money. Can this be just between the three of us?"

They both answered with a yes. "I told Lynn about this, and she told Uncle Allen, but I told her to keep it quiet. We do not want someone to think we stole it. I am going on Monday and open a savings account at the Credit Union." I will take some and put it into my checking account.

I gave each of them a fifty-dollar bill and told them to spend it on themselves.

Brian replied, I am going to fill my truck up with gas. I don't think it has ever been filled completely full.

Patty excitedly giggled; I don't know what I want to spend mine on. Think I will just keep it because I have never had a fifty-dollar bill. But I need some gas too. So I will probably fill up my truck.

They both said thank you and I could see the excitement in their eyes.

Patty and I got ready to go to church and I took some of the money to put in at church. I wrote on the outside of the envelope, Building Fund. That way it will be used on any repairs that may need done on the church. I added it to the collection plate.

Allen called me around noonish and shouted, "Hey, congratulations on your winnings or should I say, your *secret stash*. Why? Why would someone do that?"

I remarked to Allen, "I cannot imagine it. This is happening to ME! Did you ever have this happen to you with any other auctions? Has anyone found treasures at any other auctions?" I bet this is the most that anyone has found in an auction in years.

He commented, "Once in a while, people find coins or cash on things they buy at the auction like in old purses. But nothing like this! And to hoard that much cash!"

"What did they tell you when you went to the Auctioneers school about things that are found?" I asked.

He replied, "Well, it was like I told you, that all sales are final and whatever you get with your item or items belongs to the purchaser. And that would be YOU! Now if you cannot find anything to buy with it, I can take it off your hands."

I giggled and replied, "So legally it is all mine?"

"Yep! All yours," Allen replied. "Now you can go buy the kids some new comforters. Get some nice ones this time. Those were ugly."

I took some money out of the basket so that Patty and I could go to Kroger's to get some groceries. But first, we drove over to Clairbourne and went to the graveyard. I showed Patty where I buried the glass jar and she nervously said, Mom, you know I don't like graveyards. I told her I just wanted to check out the grave of the Moores. I approached the grave to find the mason jar missing. The hole was covered in with dirt. Okay, I do hope and pray that the right person took the jar and all of the papers got to the right person. What a mystery and still we don't know if the Moore girls got the papers. I can only pray that they did and that my efforts were not wasted.

We got us a sandwich to tie us over until tonight. We were out of a lot of things so off to Krogers we went. She picked out some things for her lunch next week. After getting the groceries, we went to Wal-Mart and Patty picked out a nice comforter with pillow shams. We both looked for one for Brian. Patty found one with deer on it and an outdoor scene for the background. There were two pillow shams with deer on them. We both agreed these would suit Brian since he liked the outdoors type. I bought a couple extra pillows because each of them only had one pillow for their bed.

When we got home, Brian was there and had taken his shower and was in the process of getting cleaned up and ready to go out to dinner. I took a shower when I got home then Patty took her shower. We all three got cleaned up and ready to go somewhere to eat. I took enough of the cash out of the basket to pay for our dinner. The Olive Garden sounded good but so did the Texas Roadhouse and Brian always liked the Ponderosa which was another steak house. We decided to go to the Texas Roadhouse because they both were hungry for a good steak. I do not care much for steak, so I got ribs. It was kind of noisy in the restaurant, but we managed to talk above the noise. We talked about Patty's graduation party and where and when to have it.

Patty grinned. "I don't care when it is. You don't have to have one, you know."

"Oh yes," I remarked, "we are going to have a graduation open house for you even if we must have it at our house. With this extra money, we should be able to rent the school, which is right next door or the community building in Raymond."

We talked about the stash of cash we had at home and what I was going to do with it.

I reminded them that I wanted to put some of it into the Credit Union for in case something comes up that we need it. I will put some of it in my checking account to pay some bills.

"I was able to get that credit card paid off, and I paid the taxes and got my car worked on, along with Patty's car and Brian's tires. I would take care of paying the other bills on Monday."

So maybe we can go down to Wyandot Lake and the Zoo. Or maybe to Kings Island. It has been quite some time since we were to either of these. I believe Aunt Leigh took us all one time to Kings Island. It would be nice to get several together and go to Kings Island. Leigh always liked to get a motel and stay the night. We would have to see how many are going," I told them. "We could go on a weekend, then most people would be off work."

This excited them both. "Can we bring a friend?" Brian asked.

"I guess, it depends how many are going. We may have to take my car and Leigh's van."

Brian smiled then announced, "I have this girl I want to bring. Her name is Rhonda."

Patty teased, "Brian has a girlfriend! Brian has a girlfriend!"

He swatted at her to get her to shut up.

Well, our meal was quite tasty, and we were all full, so I paid the bill, and we were homeward bound. Brian had a message from Uncle David when we got home, and he could get those tires and if Brian wanted to call him, he could go with him and get them. However, he never gave me a price.

I suggested, "Maybe you should call him in tomorrow," since it was already 9:00 p.m.

He and I bought this jacked-up truck from Uncle David. David had bought it for his son Mike but Mike found another truck. I never had to spend much money on things Brian needed.

CHAPTER 7

A New Day

We all have a past, and perhaps some were good times, and some were bad times when we had to make choices that maybe were not the best. None of us are completely innocent. As I have said before, we all get a fresh start every day to be a better person than we were yesterday.

I awoke to a beautiful morning with the sun rising over the park next door. The birds were chirping in the tree and there was the sound of a donkey's holler at the other end of town. I took my coffee out onto the patio and took in the smell of the honeysuckle and my hydrangeas close by. I love enjoying my morning coffee out onto the deck because out here, I feel closer to God and all the beauty he has created in my backyard.

Patty joined me shortly as I finished up my coffee. She brought herself out a big glass of orange juice that I had gotten at Kroger because I stocked up on things that we had been doing without. I got some doughnuts, a box of Patty's favorite cereals, and some grapes and yogurt that I thought we could eat for breakfast. So, we talked for a while as she chewed down some grapes and started eating a yogurt. I asked her about her ball games and how the school team was doing. The summer league would be starting soon, so I am sure she wanted to play summer ball again this year.

"Oh Mom! I would like to play on the Broadway team again," she answered.

"Yes, I enjoy watching you play too. Well, I will save some money back for your sign-ups. I would like to see you play for Broadway also. You do such a good job at catching. There will be other things you might need. Let us wait and see what happens this summer. This will be your last year of playing."

I told Patty that I wanted to talk to the summer ball coach and get some information. I want to donate the registration fee to the ball team to pay for a kid that did not have the money that it cost to play. If there was some child that would like to play, but their family cannot afford it, I wanted the money to go to help them. If they don't get someone, then they can use it to help buy equipment.

"This will be a good thing to do, Mom," she acknowledged and thought this was a great idea. "Maybe there will be someone in the same situation that I was in when I started playing summer ball. Thanks, Mom, that is really nice."

I cannot believe that this kind of luck has come to my family, and it has helped us in great ways and experienced some fun things in life. I got the propane tank filled up. I read somewhere that if you fill it up in the summer or fall, it is cheaper. We were so thankful that we all got new tires on our vehicles, and they were in good running condition.

We were able to rent the Broadway school on a Saturday after graduation for Patty's Graduation party. She invited lots and lots of friends and family. We invited the church families by posting the invitation on the bulletin board. It was a nice party, and she enjoyed all her family and friends that attended. I encouraged her to put some of the money she got into the Credit Union and save it for something she might need. Or she might need some money for the trip to Kings Island that we were planning for some time in July.

Her cousin Sandy graduated this year also. Sandy is her Uncle Carl's daughter. She was just four hours older than Patty. Sandy's birthday was on August 2 and Patty's was on August 3. They enjoy celebrating their birthdays each year. I am sure they will be excited to turn 18 this year.

I announced to Patty that I wanted to talk to Brian and her about a project or a plan.

"PROJECT! PLAN?" she shouted. "What kind of project do we have to do?"

"Well, go wake your brother up and I will tell you as we eat breakfast."

I fixed me another cup of coffee and got me a yogurt. I fixed the kids some things they could eat for breakfast consisting of bananas, sliced oranges, yogurt, and some doughnuts and doughnut holes. I put them on a tray and took them out onto the deck.

Brian got up shortly after and came out onto the deck and asked, "What are you doing?" Why are you waking me up so early? Why do I have to get up now and then he looked at his watch and said, Oh, I guess it is 8:30.

Patty brought with her a cup of coffee and brought Brian a glass of OJ.

I motioned to them. "Have some finger food for breakfast or there is some cereals in there."

They helped themselves to the food I had on the tray. I said, "I have been mulling over what to do with the rest of the money, so that I will feel better that I kept it."

Brian sneered. "Well, you can give me some more. I can take it off your hands."

"I know and I plan on giving you guys some of it since I have the bills paid off," I announced.

Patty heard that and sheepishly answered, "Oh boy, I cannot wait. I need some new jeans. You wouldn't buy me the ones we saw when we went shopping the other day."

I explained, "I am not buying you jeans with holes in them." She laughed and told me that I was old-fashioned.

"Well," I asked both, "have you ever heard of R A K which is Random Acts of Kindness?"

Apparently, Brian never heard of it because he asked, "What is that?"

Patty remembered that she had heard of it in Girl Scouts, but never did it.

I started to explain to them. "Say, you are at a drive-through, getting something to eat. You look behind you in your rearview mirror at the next car coming up behind you, and they have a car full of kids. Or there might be an older person or should I say elderly person behind you. Might be someone that looks grumpy or down in the dumps. After you pay for what you ordered, you pay for their order too."

Brian uttered, "I've done that before around Christmastime. I never knew it was called that."

Patty shrugged. "I seldom have enough money to pay for mine let alone someone else's."

I continued. "They would appreciate a helping hand as you pick up their bill and pay for their meal. Just ask the drive-through person to give you their bill, and you could tell her that you wanted to pay for their meal.

"You might give the drive-through people a tip when they give you your food. If you go out to eat at a restaurant, give the waiter a large tip and tell her that is her bonus. A lot of waiters rely on tips to help them make it through the week. Or even at a restaurant, you might see someone there and pay for their meal."

I went and got my Bible and Brian responded, "So are you going to preach to us, are you?"

I replied, "No, but I found a verse in my Bible. I want to read to you:

"Hebrews 13:1 and 2 read, 'Keep on loving each other as brothers. Do not forget to entertain strangers, for by so doing, some people have entertained angels without knowing it.' So," I explained some more, "this means that we should help others if we can, and it doesn't have to be poor people either. Just a little help to anyone not only makes them feel grateful but makes you feel proud of yourself that you can give them some help."

I asked, "So what about I give you each, say, one hundred dollars of that money. You go out and do several random acts of kindness. When you go through a drive-through, pay for your order and pay for the people in the car behind you."

Patty excitingly replied, "And I get to do this too?"

"Yes, you can do this and so will I. You could also go to a store and get some gift cards to some fast-food places and pass then out in the store, but then you would have to talk to the person you are giving it to. Now this is not supposed to be all your friends. I want them to be strangers too," I explained.

"Just think how this could brighten someone's day. Not only the recipient but yours also. Will you do it, guys?"

"Okay, so one hundred it is and starting today. We will talk about it at supper tonight.

"Now, these are only a few ways that RAK works. You could help someone take their groceries to their car or mow an elderly person's lawn. There are so many, I can't remember them all. But for now, let's just do the drive-through or the family at a restaurant unless an opportunity should inspire you," I explained.

I continued to tell them, "This may only take five to ten minutes of your day, but you will have enlightened someone's day for a long, long time. Kindness circles around, you know. Paying it forward is not an issue, it is a behavioral choice. I try to be kind to others, regardless of whether they have been kind to me. We all have bad days and might not treat others well. Remember that when someone is not nice to you—maybe they are just having a bad day and sometimes it's best to just walk away."

The next day, the kids came home, and they had done a few acts of kindness, and they were eager to talk about it. Brian went through McDonalds and paid for the elderly lady that came up behind him in the drive-through. He told how she tooted her horn at him and rolled down her window and waved at him.

Patty explained that she went through the coffee place she likes, and the line was so long. She looked behind her in the line and there were two young ladies behind her. She told the lady at the window of the drive-through that she wanted to pay for the car behind her. The lady replied, "You want to do what?" She told the lady again that she wanted to pay for whatever the car behind her got and pay for her coffee. The lady told her that it was nice of you to do that. As she was pulling away, they honked and waved at her as they were leaving. She noticed on the bill that they bought two of the big muffins plus some specialty coffees.

She commented, "Mom, I felt so good doing that."

"Well, listen to this," I announced. "I was in the local grocery store and I paid for mine then I waited till this older lady behind me got checked out. I believe she had lunchmeat and cheese and a package of probably hamburger. It was all wrapped in that white paper so you could not see what was in it. She had some bread and milk, Oreo, and some potatoes. It totaled thirty-five dollars plus some change. I paid for her groceries and helped her carry them out to her car. She thanked me all the way out to the car. I told her good-bye and God bless you and she whispered, 'God bless you too, honey,' and finally got into her car."

The kids continued with their random acts of kindness as did I. Doing RAK not only has a direct effect on others but has a positive impact on yourself as well.

Brian confessed, he went and got a bunch of quarters and put them in the pop machine at work but did not select. He stood back and watched as people came up and put their money in and made their selection and their drink came out and so did a bunch of quarters. They were excited and confused. This guy turned around and bought the person behind him a drink with the free money he had.

"It was kind of amusing to watch them," he laughingly replied.

I announced as I pulled out an envelope from my pocket and in it, I had a few gift cards. "Look in here and take one of each, then go out and pass them out. I went and bought some fifteen-dollar gift cards for the local fast-food places and some for local eating places. I thought I would pass them out at the grocery store and maybe you could pass them out at your ballgames, Patty. I got a couple from the hair salons, and I passed them out at the Food Pantry."

Patty came home from the school ball practice and was eager to tell me about her RAK. She explained, the coaches took them to get ice cream after practice and she paid for all of them. She thought that some of them did not have any money on them. Most of them got milkshakes and some got Sundays. She told me, "Mom, I felt so good that I could do that. All the girls thanked me. I even bought drinks for the coaches."

"I am so proud of you, girl!" I shouted "Now it does make you feel good when you can make someone's day a little brighter. So would you continue to do it on occasion?" She agreed that she would probably do it again.

I asked Brian, "Would you do this again and in days to come?"

He replied, "Yes, I probably will do it again on occasion."

I started the kids off with some extra cash in their pockets, and we agreed that since I got all the bills paid up and all our vehicles were in better running condition, we will work on getting the family together and go to Kings Island for a vacation.

Several weeks later, after the excitement had died down and things got back to routine, we were able to relax. After supper one evening, I was done with the dishes and both the kids were home that night. Patty had enjoyed her new comforter on her bed and was enjoying sleeping on top of it most of the time. Brian was pleased with his comforter that we picked out for his bed. For a while, they both kept their bed made up but that soon wore off as time passed.

I always tried to teach my children to be sensitive about other people's feelings. I think it is important to show compassion not only for family, but for friends and other people as well.

One morning, I awoke early to a rainy morning. I was sitting by the kitchen table, nurturing my cup of coffee, and paying some bills. Brian just happened to be looking for something in his closet. He came across the shams from the old comforter. He brought his shams out to me and laid one on the table with my bills and held the other in his arms. I asked, "Do you want me to put those in the tote with

Patty's? I'm not sure what we should do with them." "Clip the corner on the top," Brian requested. "That will be your answer," he said.

It was designed with patches of materials on top with a small ruffle around the edge just like the comforter. It did have a very faint smell of coffee even though I washed it when I washed the comforters several months ago. It was made to resemble the comforter.

With a twinkle in his eye, Brian took the scissors and handed them to me and pointed to the patchwork top sham, and asked, "Do you want to check them out or should I?" There are four of them.

And that will be for the next story.

I only fantasized that I would write a book, and yet here we are, at the end of my first novel. Now that we have gotten here, I feel even more grateful for the opportunity I've had to reach out through these pages and touched your heart. Authoring this book has made me more aware of the people who have touched my heart, my mind and in so doing, nurtured my soul.

I hope you enjoyed all the incidents in my story. Perhaps you will be inspired to go to auctions and love them as much as I do. Maybe you might even practice the RAK giving sometime. I am anxious to go to another auction and will continue to enjoy all the people there, and all my family that attends. I am planning to write another story in the near future.

Be careful about all the obstacles in your life. They happen for a reason and may strengthen you as you continue in your life's journey. I am blessed and lucky because I believe that God has personally watched over me through all of my life each and every day. My journey continues and I am awaiting the next 20 years.

It is so hard for me to believe that I am now an author of this book.

THE SURPRISE AUCTION

This book is a work of fiction. Some of the items are true and some are not. Some of the names and characters have been changed. Some of the places and incidents are the product of the author's imagination or are used fictitiously. Any resemblance to actual events, locales, or persons, living or dead, is coincidental.

To my mother, Clara Belle Rosebrook, I dedicate this book. She has always supported my writings for the newspaper. She always looked forward to reading my next article. Whenever I would write about our family events, she would cut the article out and put it in a scrapbook. We found three huge scrapbooks of her clippings while sorting through her treasured items after her passing.

Thank You

I wish to thank all my family members for their help in completing this book. They are Ken and Renee Rosebrook who supported me when I said I wanted to write a book. Mary Rosebrook who read my first transcript before my book was completed and always found a way to positively contribute. And my daughter Patty Galloway that read my book when I first started writing and gave me the strength to pursue it. I would like to thank my dear friends Lorna Mathys and Donna Dafler for having faith in me and persuading me to complete my heart's desire and complete my first book. Thank you all for supporting me so I could successfully make my wish come true.

Thanks to all of you.
Ruth Giles
"Starling Rose"